"Charge!" came the cry. "Charge the blockhouse!"

Amid the chaos of battle, with men and horses falling all around him, young Brian Dexter Cook could still make out the stocky, bespectacled figure of Colonel Teddy Roosevelt urging his men forward. The blockhouse atop San Juan Hill, heavily defended, must be taken if the battle was to be won.

Brian felt himself and his mount carried on a relentless forward surge. He himself was firing his carbine at anything that moved, so long as it was wearing a sombrero. He saw his friend, Richard Harding Davis, still unharmed, riding behind Teddy Roosevelt, who had discarded his saber and was now firing his big horse pistol.

And then, behind him, Brian caught sight of Sergeant Harkness, grim smile on his cruel face, raising his carbine. And in that split second, Brian knew that the deadliest enemy was not up ahead of him on the hill, but directly behind him . . .

## The Making of America Series

# THE
# ROUGH
# RIDERS

Lee Davis Willoughby

A DELL/JAMES A. BRYANS BOOK

Published by
Dell Publishing Co., Inc.
1 Dag Hammarskjold Plaza
New York, New York 10017

Dell ® TM 681510, Dell Publishing Co., Inc.

ISBN: 0-440-07549-1

Printed in the United States of America

First printing—November 1984

For
William James Daprato,
Sept. 22, 1921–Nov. 30, 1983,
who would have charged up San Juan Hill
with Colonel Teddy and me.
God rest, Dap, until we meet again.
When all the bugles sound *Retreat*.

# THE ROUGH RIDERS

# BOOK ONE

## THE GATHERING OF EAGLES
## IN ANGER

". . . by thunder, Brian, the Cuban rebels have been revolting against tyrannical Spanish rule since 'ninety-five and it is clearly up to righteous thinking Americans to lend them a hand! We should prepare for war against Spain now—this very day—before something calamitous happens. I am impatient with that man in the White House, my boy. What in the name of blue blazes is McKinley waiting for? Another *Maine* going down in Havana harbor? I tell you that man has no more backbone than a chocolate éclair. . . ."

> —*Theodore Roosevelt, Assistant Secretary of the Navy, April 19th, 1898, Capitol Hill cloak room, among friends.*

## "REMEMBER THE MAINE!"

On February 15, 1898, in the Spanish port of Havana, Cuba, the United States battleship *Maine* squatted peacefully at anchor. The mighty behemoth of the seas had arrived at the picturesque docking point on the day of January the twenty-fifth. Its important mission had been anything but peaceful. Armed Cuban rebels, in open defiance of tormenting Spanish rule, had swept down from the surrounding hills to threaten the city. To protect American lives and property, President William

McKinley had dispatched the *Maine* to guard and uphold U.S. interests. It was an executive decision admired and seconded throughout the youngest country in the world. Yet the presence of the mighty *Maine* in Havana Harbor was to prove the catalyst for an impending conflict no one had bargained for. Or dreamed possible.

Were you on the lovely shore that day, enjoying the warm tropical sunlight and contrasting cool winds, you would have experienced the shock of a lifetime. Something to remember always.

The *Maine* riding idly at anchor, white sea gulls plucking the refuse of the harbor in organized flight, the great sun boiling down, ship's bells sounding to mark the change of watch, and smaller, lesser craft bobbing and cruising in the placid green waters, and then—a mammoth explosion shatters the stillness of the day. Great columns of dark, ugly smoke spiral upwards from the massive battleship. Men can be seen running on her plated decks. There is a great tumult of shouting, yelling, and screaming. Then another explosion, a lesser one, but the effect is equally disastrous. The gigantic vessels lists to one side like a stricken animal. Climbing flames from the stern spread magically across the bows. The tall, sturdy mast shudders, plates buckle, and a series of smaller detonations sound. The giant machine, the pride of the United States Navy, slowly and inexorably settles into the depths of Havana Harbor. Going down like an enormous rock dropped into the sea.

Within a time so short it defies all logic and realization, the *USS Maine* sinks, only its tall mast, complete with crow's nest and radio antennae, sticking up from the green waters to mark the spot where it has grown down. A victim of some nebulous act.

More than two hundred sixty of the crew members have gone to a watery grave.

In the hectic days that followed the disaster, which rocks the English-speaking world, a naval court of inquiry concludes that a submarine mine caused the explosion. The United States openly accuses Spain of willful, premeditated aggression. Spain defends herself on the grounds that an explosion inside the ship itself caused the catastrophe. There is vast anger and hatred on both sides.

The calamitous event, however, is not to be glossed over.

Officially, the United States government does not move. Or act. No country can go off half-cocked in emergencies. It is not the way of government, of rational, thinking law-makers. The consequences, the intangibles and the imponderables, must be measured before a country can take up arms and fight.

And yet, Public Opinion is perhaps the mightiest weapon of all—the single sine qua non by which most wars and conflicts are triggered. America and Americans were angry. Something had to feed that anger, fan it, flame it, spur the nation into action.

Finally, ultimately. To total commitment.

The great newspaper world took over, as it always does—those town criers, those vigilantes of vengeance, those makers of wars. America would and could be heard on the terrible subject of foreign countries killing American subjects without paying the piper.

The awesome machinery of William Randolph Hearst's *New York Journal*, Joseph Pulitzer's *The New York World*, James Gordon Bennett's *New York Herald*, and the literally hundreds of news papers and magazines throughout the United States, from the jagged shores of Maine to California, took up the cudgels for justice and demanded immediate action. Retribution for wicked Spain and its hordes. The battleship that went down in Havana Harbor was not to be dismissed and never to be forgotten. It would be immortalized for all posterity.

*Remember the* Maine! became the battle cry of the United States of America, the tocsin for action, the spur for the future.

Its direct result was the Spanish-American War.

President McKinley and Congress demanded the liberation of Cuba from Spanish rule. Spain refused.

McKinley and Congress insisted on the withdrawal of Spain from Cuba. Again, refusal.

The outcome was inevitable. Bold headlines were coming up.

On April 24, 1898, the United States formally declared that a state of war existed between the U.S. and Spain.

Thus, the Spanish-American War.

Marking the emergence of the United States of America was a world power, it was to be a war that everyone wanted. Everyone in America, that is.

Everyone had remembered the *Maine*. All too well.

No small thanks was owed to the universe of newspapers and newspapermen. Hearst, Pulitzer, and Bennett had not slept on the matter.

Neither had Brian Dexter Cook.

Another newspaperman—with a mission. Two missions.

Missions that had little to do with remembering a battleship which had gone down in Havana Harbor.

# *DELMONICO'S AND DECISIONS*

They came to Delmonico's in waves every evening. They came in dress suits, evening gowns, diamonds, stickpins—all the glittering, golden people of New York. For this landmark restaurant in old Manhattan was a mecca for the rich, the well-informed, and any and all who were important in the scheme of things. With the eighteen ninety-eight calendar year clearly indicating that the nineteenth century was about to give way to the twentieth, Delmonico's was surely the place to dine, the place to be, when history and great events were in the offing. Civilization was on the march. And Delmonico's was marching with it. So all carriages and hansom cabs pointed their horses toward the lavish dining kingdom which had dominated the cobbled environs of lower Gotham for decades.

Tonight was no exception.

Indeed, on this May evening, the Delmonico milieu was heightened with excitement; the hubbub and metropolitan roar and rhythm was doubled. The declaration of war against Spain had produced twice as many denizens and habitués of the historic restaurant. The entrance to the place was a procession of cabs and carriages and busy doormen and bristling patrons. The top-hatted clientele and their bejeweled ladies for the evening were out in force. There was a full moon overhead, riding in the Manhattan skies, but no one saw it. The glare of the fashionable facade with its rows of electric lights shaded in chandelier form seemed to blot out the rest of the world. Edison's great discovery and invention was nearly twenty years of age, but Delmonico's still seemed a candlelit universe. Old World, as it were, with the best that Europe had to offer and the finest American touches. Everyone loved Delmonico's.

Within the lavish interior, the tables and booths were filled to overflowing. All kinds of voices and all sorts of accents mingled in a babel that might

go on forever. Blue cigar smoke wafted and cham-
pagne glasses clinked; dishes clattered as liveried
waiters moved to and fro, walking silently and
efficiently, while the monied patrons cared not a
feather or a fig for the uproar they were creating.
War was in the air; the United States was flexing its
young muscles, and not since the Civil War had
Yankee arms been tested in battle. This time it
would not be brother-against-brother. No, Henry.
This was American might against a foreign tyrant!

The women in their evening gowns of silver and
gold, with fur coats of mink, ermine, and sable very
much in evidence, were thrilled and titillated with the
talk of the men at their tables. In truth, history was in
the making, and all felt a part of it. Thank the
Lord—the President, Congress, and the country
had finally decided to do something dramatic about
that awful sinking of the poor *Maine*. And all
those dead boys on board—God Bless William
McKinley of Niles, Ohio, the twenty-fifth president of these United States. A Republican, if you
please, as true and blue as the Grand Old Party.
The elephant was on a rampage á là Thomas Nast's
art.

Far back in the crowded restaurant, at a discreet
corner table in one of the leather upholstered booths,
two men sat in solemn conclave. They had hardly
touched their dinners—Delmonico's fine steaks á
là the French chef—and now seemed only interested in their drinks, a Bordeaux table wine of

excellent vintage. The fact that both men were
dining without female companionship on such a
night in such a fashionable dining room might
have' elicited comment. For they were very easily
the two handsomest men in Delmonico's that
evening. In fact, one of them was no less than
Richard Harding Davis, the premier newspaperman
of the day. Dick Davis, the daring, the intrepid,
the man who had carved out a name and reputation for himself with Charles A. Dana's *Evening
Sun, Harper's Magazine*, and hosts of stories and
pieces about rich people. New York knew him as a
convivial, clever, young man about town, but his
byline had become star material wherever it
appeared. When he rode with the U.S. Cavalry in
'92 in their pursuit of Mexican revolutionaries, his
dispatches from the seat of his horse handed the
resounding lie to all those who had claimed that
Dick Davis could only write a headline story from
a table in Delmonico's. At the remarkably young
age of thirty-five, he was already a celebrity. And
now the Spanish-American War had come and the
Hearst papers had commissioned him to cover the
action for them. He was going to be paid to go
where the story was breaking—the hotbed, Cuba.
Richard Harding Davis was the newspaperman every young buck fresh out of a journalism course in
college wanted to be in eighteen hundred and
ninety-eight.

Except the young man seated across from him in

the quiet corner table at Delmonico's. Brian Dexter Cook only listened to the sound of his own drum, and indeed walked to a different drummer. This, in truth, was the major reason that Richard Harding Davis loved his company. He had had his fill of fawning tyroes, mercenary friends, and adoring females with little in their heads save feathers.

Both men, taken at a glance, and then studied, might have served as models for the typical American male of the day. They were both six-footers, clean-cut, without the handlebar moustache or mutton-chop whiskers or chin beards then in fashion. Both wore identical four-button, wide-lapeled dark brown woolen suits, crested with white starched collar and matching tie studded with a stickpin. But whereas Davis' ornament was a genuine diamond, Cook's was imitation. And the bowler hat and white gloves tucked in one corner of the booth were the property of Davis. Brian Dexter Cook did not wear a hat—ever: an idiosyncracy that marked him in any crowd.

Davis was full-jawed and dark-eyed with bushy black brows; he had an air of acute alertness about him that impressed an onlooker and all that he met. Brian Dexter Cook was a blue-eyed, smoothly bronzed, straight-nosed, firm-lipped young man, whose cascade of golden blonde hair always fluttered in a morning or evening breeze. But for all his outdoors look, there was a grimness about his features, an uncompromising cast to his eyes that was most commanding—an aura that Richard Harding Davis still remembered from their very first encounter in front of the Flatiron Building on East Twenty-Third Street when the foundation was being laid for what was to be Manhattan's tallest building. That had only been last year, but Davis had been surprised to learn that the young cub was also working at Hearst's offices. Indeed, Brian Dexter Cook already had a byline, thanks to a heart-felt, well-written piece about sweatshops in the Garment District that employed children as young as seven years of age. Davis had liked that piece; he liked Cook even better, and they became fast friends. The way Cook had taken some pokes and jibes at the Industrial Revolution, which had caused such horrors, indicated a mind far beyond his years. Richard Harding Davis loved the company of brilliant people. Brian Dexter Cook struck him as a real newcomer to the profession of journalism. One worth watching.

"See here, you young ass—" Davis suddenly broke the silence that had lasted far too long between them since they had abandoned their steaks. "You've already spoiled my appetite. Now don't go and spoil your career. And your life. Do what the Old Man tells you."

"I can't, Dick. I honestly can't. Don't think I haven't considered the alternatives. I have. I know I should leap at the chance to work with you on this Cuban assignment, but I just can't—"

"Your reasons aren't good enough," Davis said firmly, but in a kindly way. "Simply because you don't admire your publisher is no good answer. Good God—do you think Melba loves every song she sings at the Met? I'm sure she doesn't, but she sings them all the same."

Brian Dexter Cook smiled, and the transformation in his young, handsome face was incredible. He was suddenly boyish, vulnerable.

"The analogy will not serve, you word wizard. It's principle, not product. And it certainly isn't art, either. How can I cover a war assignment for a man I believe practically started that war?"

Richard Harding Davis snorted in a refined, elegant way—ever the gentleman. "That's nonsense, and you know it. William Randolph Hearst is responsible neither for the sinking of the *Maine* nor for the way in which the Spanish government treats its people, not to mention its rebels. Come off it, Brian. That's schoolboy talk. This is the big world; learn to live in it. It's the opportunity of a lifetime for you. Cuba will be glory for both of us. Wait and see."

"I couldn't agree with you more. I am certainly going to Cuba. But not with you. Nor for Mister Hearst. I've accepted James Gordon Bennett's offer. I'm covering this thing for *The New York Herald.* And I won't have to write scare headlines or shade the news or editorialize to please my boss." Brian

Dexter Cook spoke his piece quietly, but even he was aware of what he was saying and implying.

Davis had stiffened a trifle, but then he smiled and shook his head. "I don't know why I bless you with my company, you young scalawag. You're as much as telling me that I will take Hearst money, no matter the principle, thereby compromising my—art, shall I say?—well, you couldn't be wronger, my idealistic young comrade. You miss the point entirely. What I will write is still my business. Even as I accept Hearst money, Hearst prestige, and Hearst bounty. Do I make myself clear? I respect your decision, kindly respect and understand mine. I am still working for myself. Remember that."

Cook's face crumpled apologetically.

"Forgive me, Dick. I didn't mean it the way it sounded."

"You're a fine writer, Brian. But you don't know it all yet. Remember that. Those adverbs and adjectives must be properly placed or your meaning will be taken wrong. More wine?"

"I'd be honored."

"I, too. But not for the same reasons."

All about them, the restaurant babel continued with scarcely a break in volume. At surrounding tables, females, though clearly with male escorts, were casting glances in their direction—glances both admiring and coquettish. Davis nodded to one of these, saluting her with his wineglass before sipping. Brian Dexter Cook, while not exactly a connoisseur of beautiful women, still marveled at the stir his famous friend always caused in public places.

"The cynosure of all eyes, Dick. That is most certainly you."

"It's a bore sometimes. But it does get me the best tables in restaurants. And sometimes I do get lucky and meet a real pippin."

Cook laughed. "There's a pippin over there. The brunette with the bearded man. She keeps eyeing you from behind her fan."

"Let her eye. You're all the company I want this night. And since we haven't done justice to Pierre's magnificent filet mignons, what excuse can we give when it comes time for me to pay the check?"

"Charge it up to war nerves. Too excited to eat, and so forth."

"Not bad. A trifle lame, but not bad. He just might believe that, considering the state of high fever everyone seems to be in at dear old Delmonico's tonight." Davis pyramided his hands after setting his wineglass down gently on the snow-white tablecloth. "Did you know that Steve Crane's in town? Staying at the Ansonia. Saw him yesterday. He has some idea of enlisting in the Navy for this go-round."

"*The Red Badge of Courage*," Cook murmured fervently. "Read that three times at Cornell. It's amazing he could write a book like that without ever having seen the Civil War."

"Why amazing?" David scoffed. "He's a talented writer—he has imagination. Just knew how to use it, that's all. Do you know him personally, by the way?"

"We've never met, though I'd consider such a meeting an honor."

"I'll arrange it then. Before we all shove off for points below America. He'll never make the Navy, though. He's thin as a rail and paler than Hamlet's ghost. Still, any paper would be glad to have him cover this campaign for them. He has all the tools— and a name to boot." Richard Harding Davis paused meaningfully. "So you're going to write for the opposition. James Gordon Bennett—the Old Man will have fits when he hears that."

"He knows already. And he had them this morning when he fairly ordered me out of his office. Which was when I phoned the *Herald*. Mr. Bennett hired me on the spot. Seems he knew of me—my work, at any rate—and was impressed. I sail for Cuba on the seventh. Officially. Haven't worked out all the details yet."

"Well, you're forthright and honest, at least. I'll say that for you. You didn't get the job with the *Herald* first and then make your little speech to William Randolph. Wish I'd been there. That owl face of his must have been something to see. He turns nearly purple when he's angry—did he turn purple, Brian?''

"Like the Grand Canyon at sunset, Richard—''

There was an untimely interruption. A quite unexpected one that caught both men completely off guard. Lurching toward them from one of the nearby tables, pushing angrily despite the efforts of a lovely, brunette-haired companion to check him, was a tall, massive, florid-faced man in evening clothes, whose unsteady gait clearly told the tale of too much indulgence in the grape. Both Davis and Cook tensed in their chairs, but the encounter was unavoidable.

"You call yourselves gentlemen?'' came the loud, angry challenge in a deep basso which could be heard within twenty feet of their table. "Well, that's not what I call you, you muckraking scoundrels! Filthy scribblers—the pack of you! Putting lies on paper, that's all you're good for—plunging this country into a war it has no business fighting—''

Instant silence, as if everyone in Delmonico's had been immobilized and frozen into ice, descended magically over the area. Not a glass clinked; not a fork or spoon rattled. Not a soul stirred. All heads swung toward the far end of the room and the corner table where Mr. Richard Harding Davis and his unknown companion were about to be accosted, or confronted, or worse, by a well-dressed stranger. Certainly not one of Delmonico's regulars—he would never have been so crude, so ill-mannered, and *de trop*, as the French like to say.

Even the army of waiters and serving people seemed paralyzed with the awkwardness and uncouthness of the moment. Time had stopped.

Richard Harding Davis placed his hands to either side of his body, palms down to the table. His cool eyes stared upward at the swaying, snarling giant before him. His shoulders tautened.

"Sir, you have us at a disadvantage. We have never met."

"Damn right we haven't, Davis! I wouldn't care to be seen with the likes of you and your friend there! Reporters, eh? Bunch of mealy-mouthed gossips, that's what you are! Picking on McKinley, setting down every name that Teddy Roosevelt has called him—until you finally got what you set out to do! War, by God, that's what! You ought to be run out of town on a rail—you damned meddlers. Muckraking, warmongering scum! You and that boss of yours, Mr. William Randolph Hearst—"

The lovely brunette behind him moaned into her clasped hands, her dark, exquisite eyes as round and white as moons.

Richard Harding Davis rose from his chair and reached for his white gloves. He began to put them on, quietly, easily, while the red-faced, drunken man continued to swear invective and wrath. Brian Dexter Cook did not rise, but he never took his eyes off his target. His icy blue eyes were unblinking.

Davis reached for his cane. "If you've quite finished, I think the time has come to thrash you publicly. It might teach you a lesson. When ladies are present, language such as yours, sir, is not to be tolerated—"

He had misjudged his man or simply erred on the interpretation of the drunken outburst. For with abrupt speed and an amazing amount of vengeful determination, the angry giant swung a vicious, hard-handed fist at Richard Harding Davis' head, which was half-inclined in the act of picking up the walking stick. The brunette woman shrieked in fright. Davis ducked, but he would have been too late by seconds—if Brian Dexter Cook had not intervened in a manner most precipitous and altogether magnificent. It was the sort of Horatio Alger stunt that small boys all over the United States admired and hoped to emulate one day.

Before the cruel, heavy hand could land—it would have injured Davis severely if it had—Brian Dexter Cook vaulted over the well-set table in a flying leap, both arms extended in a parabola of grace. It was the kind of well-coordinated athletic feat that only a trained gymnast could have executed. And execute it Cook did. In flying moments, he had caught the red-faced, massive man across the chest, broken the direction of his traveling right arm, and borne him to the floor in a heap. Heavily. Cook landed atop the downed aggressor, but the man outweighed him by at least seventy-five pounds.

The intoxicated swell rumbled in his chest, shook Cook off, and lumbered to his feet—quite like a bulldog shaking off a terrier. But with all that, he was still no match for the lighter, lither man he had triggered into action. Richard Harding Davis could only look on, his jaw dropped in wonder, his hand still clutching his rattan cane.

The massive, broad-shouldered drunk hurled a hamlike hand at Brian Dexter Cook. Another woman screamed in Delmonico's. Somebody else shouted for order to be restored. Cook restored it in less time than it took for Richard Harding Davis to describe what happened next to rapt listeners the next day in the Hearst offices.

Cook's head dropped to his chest as his left arm lashed out to block the oncoming fist, and then he shifted and his own right fist came forward in a straight-from-the-shoulder punch. Everyone in Delmonico's saw what happened next. And heard it, too. A mighty *thuck* of sound, like two sides of beef being slapped together, and then the drunk's head snapped back and down he went. He hit the deeply carpeted floor and stayed there. He did not move. The offending mouth was closed, at last.

And from that moment forward, Delmonico's was uproar itself.

There was a burst of applause, shouts of "Bravo! Bravo!" and a rush of patrons in evening gowns and dinner clothes in the direction of the Harding table. Waiters hurried to help; Davis himself led the ovation with an orchestra conductor's flourish—his handsome, good-natured face wreathed in a smile that would eclipse the sun. Brian Dexter Cook stood his ground, kneeling beside the man he had bested so completely to make certain the ape was only unconscious and not badly hurt. And the lovely brunette, now a concerned vision in a blue-flowered dress, was pressing his arm anxiously, her oval, lovely face upturned to him. "Oh, please . . . is he all right? . . . He shouldn't have said all those beastly things. . . . it's not like him, really . . ."

"That was no way to talk to anyone—who is he?"

"My Uncle Waldo. He's ever so gentle when he doesn't drink too much—please, help me get him to the table."

"All right. I'm sorry I had to hit him. But he could have killed Dick."

"I know, I know. It wasn't your fault—anyone could see that—"

In the midst of all the hubbub and the furore, Richard Harding Davis quickly organized things and restored order. The contretemps, the awkward moment, was done, but already news was on the wing; scandal and sensation were being paid tribute to. On hand in Delmonico's that May night was a pair of reporters from the *New York World* who were even then on the telephone, scooping

Richard Harding Davis and Brian Dexter Cook. New York would awaken in the morning to learn, as they digested their coffee and rolls, that two of Mr. William Randolph Hearst's prize byliners had defended the honor of the fourth estate by thoroughly trouncing one Mr. Waldo Friedlinger. Mr. Friedlinger, it would turn out, was no less than a principal stockholder in the Bates Bible Company. This, it seemed, completely explained and justified Mr. Friedlinger's stance about war and newspapers—though it did not explain his overindulgence in alcohol. The *World* would further cite the presence of Mr. Friedlinger's niece during the brawl. Miss Linda Balfour, exceedingly attractive, was enjoying a visit with her uncle in his Fifth Avenue manor while, on holiday from her normal occupation as school librarian in Lake Placid, upstate New York. She, too, was a pacifist.

Thus, another night in the famous Delmonico's.

Another headline-making news story in the Manhattan manner.

So Richard Harding Davis laughingly and succinctly put it on the carriage ride that took him and Cook back to their respective lodgings that night, for he had quickly spotted Larrabee and Wilson of the *World* racing for the telephones in the downstairs lounge at Delmonico's:

"Let's face the facts, Brian my boy. We have been *scooped*."

Brian Dexter Cook laughed, too.

He did not care.

Miss Linda Balfour had given him her phone number, asking him to call on her the next day. Behind Uncle Waldo's back, of course. Who would be off to his club in the West Fifties, nursing his wounds.

The oval face with the earnest, appealing eyes promised much in the way of reward for young Galahads who assisted damsels in distress.

For one day at least, the war could be forgotten, put aside.

The war that was to change his own life so drastically.

Change it for all the years to come.

As it would for so many men and women, American and Spanish, in the war-torn months to follow.

And for the record, let it be stated that in eighteen hundred and ninety-eight, William Randolph Hearst was merely in his mid-thirties. Still, by all measures, a young man.

But to everyone, friend and foe alike, he was the Old Man of newspaper publishing.

One who knew all there was to know about running a newspaper.

And the great purposes to which it could be put.

*Vox populi*, indeed. The Voice of the People.

It was a policy that would lead to *yellow journalism*.

Linking William Randolph Hearst to the indelible image of a man "who would print anything to sell newspapers."

There was never any question of taste.

Good or bad.

Nor even of right or wrong.

An issue Brian Dexter Cook had had no doubts about since the day he was born in Staten Island, New York.

# MANILA BAY AND MEN

On the following day, May the second, America awoke to electrifying news. No small thanks to Marconi's wireless system and the efficiency of relay stations and geared-to-transmit telegraph outposts, the newest and most sensational development in the Spanish-American War became ready information for the world. The United States of America numbered forty-five in '98 because the Arizona, New Mexico, and Oklahoma territories had not as yet cast their lot with the Union Forever.

There were forty-five stars on the Grand Old Flag
and something like seventy-two million people who
called themselves citizens—who truly had something to crow about and take pride in: American
arms had won the day in the very first engagement
of the conflict.

Dewey at Manila was the talk of the town. And
the globe.

The details, the fine points, the meat of the
victory was there for everyone to read in the *Herald*,
the *World*, the *Journal*, and all the tabloids, gazettes,
and dailies in existence.

America, McKinley's administration and the people themselves, had taken a mighty step forward.
Upward, as a world power.

George Dewey, American naval officer, was the
hero of the hour—the right man at the right place
and certainly at the right time. Behaviorally, he
could not have been surpassed. Not ever.

A little more than a week earlier, when war had
erupted between Spain and the United States, Dewey
had been in command of the Asiatic fleet in Hong
Kong. On direct orders from the War Department
and the President, he had proceeded with dispatch
for the Philippine Islands—to capture or destroy
the Spanish fleet harbored there. Never has any
military personage obeyed instructions so well.
Late on the afternoon of April the thirtieth, Dewy's
six ships, spearheaded by his own *USS Olympia*,
steamed into Manila Bay. A Spanish fleet of ten

cruisers and gunboats lay in wait for him. The initial engagement of the war was at hand.

"You may fire when ready, Gridley," Dewey commanded his subordinate. It was the sentence heard around the world, the sentence spoken on the morning of May the first, that would echo down the halls of history.

Dewey and his six ships launched their attack, flags flying, deck guns thundering. The air was alive with the sounds of combat.

And before twelve noon that day, Dewey had accomplished the miraculous and near-impossible with great seamanship and courage.

The entire Spanish Fleet had been bested, destroyed, and sent to the bottom of the bay— without the loss of a single American life! The American flag, Old Glory, fluttered triumphantly in Manila Bay. And there it would fly and there it would stay with Dewey and his vessels standing guard until ground troops would arrive to capture and hold Manila.

Dewey's victory would make the United States an important power in the Pacific Ocean. The American people had found a newer and greater pride and confidence in the U.S. Navy.

George Dewey, naval officer, was truly the Man of the Hour.

The Gay Nineties was never gayer than that day of May the second. Now had come the time to dance in the streets again, to sing the songs of

America, to jump up and down in national joy. To shout the praises of all things American. Life was good again.

The nation's newspapers had a field day.

Patriotism was once again a shining word.

And Richard Harding Davis packed his bags, readied his assortment of writing equipment, and prepared to take the next boat out to hasten to Cuba. To be where the action was. To fulfill his contract with publisher William Randolph Hearst. And Destiny.

And Brian Dexter Cook, all unknowing, hailed a passing hansom cab, smiling in amusement as one of Henry Ford's experimental automobiles stalled in heavy traffic on Fourteenth Street. Cook was on his way uptown to see once again Miss Linda Balfour. They had an appointment for lunch together, within the luxurious walls of Uncle Waldo's Fifth Avenue manor. Choleric Uncle Waldo would be at his club. At least, that was what Miss Balfour had promised. Shyly, demurely.

Brian Dexter Cook was as anxious as Dick Davis to get to Cuba, to get the job done, to see at first hand what the America Navy and Army had accomplished and would accomplish. But that would have to wait. His boat would not sail for a week yet—the steamboat *Marlboro*.

He was as excited as everyone in town, and the world, about Dewey's victory, but he was also a very young man.

Now was the time for romance. And the thrill of being alone with a most attractive young lady. A possible damsel in distress.

At Cornell University, by old Cayuga's waters, as the song went, Brian Dexter Cook had majored in journalism and English literature. He had sampled all the classic writers, from William Shakespeare to Thackeray to Charles Dickens. But he had also wolfed down Scott's *Ivanhoe*, Dumas' *The Three Musketeers*, Cooper's *The Last of the Mohicans*, and most of Twain, Whitman, Emerson, and Hawthorne.

The plain, unvarnished truth was that Brian Dexter Cook was an incorrigible romantic, for all his smooth, poker-faced demeanor. The icy blue eyes were a lie. He was a flesh-and-blood male.

His mother had been a lithographer who had worked for Currier and Ives, his father a Staten Island ferryman. They had both worked all their lives to see to it that he earned a college education. The terrible accident which had claimed them both only five short years ago—the collapse of a faulty bridge in the borough of the Bronx while they were on a visit to Emily Plank Cook's parents— had only strengthened Brian's resolve to make something of himself and to tell the truth always as a journalist. The bridge had only fallen because inferior materials had gone into its construction. Graft had been paid to the contractor who won the bid. Human rights had been ignored.

Thus, Brian Dexter Cook, newspaperman and idealist, was a bit of a rebel against taking the easy way out or doing things as everyone else did because "that's the way things are. Why fight City Hall?"

Brian would fight. Always. To his last breath.

But on this May day, none of these things were on his mind.

Miss Linda Belfour was waiting. Brunette, oval-faced, red-lipped.

A veritable pippin, as Richard Harding Davis would affirm and agree in his straightforward, no-nonsense manner.

The sun was high in the Manhattan heavens as Brian Dexter Cook's hansom cab clip-clopped uptown. Manhattan had a festive air.

Under his breath, barely conscious of the act, he was tunefully humming "My Wild Irish Rose." He had a good ear for a tune.

It was one of the song hits of the day. The sheet music for the melody was literally a sell-out daily at Harms Music Publishers, Incorporated. Everybody wanted to play the piece on their pianos.

Miss Lillian Russell, she of the hourglass figure and ample charms, was the toast of Broadway, singing "My Wild Irish Rose."

Brian Dexter Cook would have given her little competition.

Neither would have Diamond Jim Brady, her consort.

Miss Lillian was in a class by herself.

A nonpareil. A one-of-a-kind.

Like George Dewey was this day.

An all-American to the teeth, by God!


"You wanted to see me, Mr. Hearst?"

"Come in, Miss Weatherall. And do shut the door. There's a nasty draft from that hallway—something I can't understand, considering how much money I paid to build this place."

"Yes, sir."

"Take that chair, the one across from me. I want to look at you. I've heard you were the most beautiful woman who works for me. I confess, I want to see for myself."

"Really, Mr. Hearst—"

"Now, now, Weatherall. No timidity. I won't have it. You're a newspaperman? Act like one. Look me in the eye and don't turn away. I'm about to present you with the opportunity of your lifetime. Live up to the moment, woman. Don't retreat."

"All right. I won't, if you say I shouldn't. But please—I'm not accustomed to being stared at as though I were a box of bonbons in a shop window. It's rather—disconcerting."

William Randolph Hearst guffawed. His owl-eyed face, with its long, peaked nose and severe mouth, was uncharacteristically creased with amusement. He pointed a live forefinger across the massive desk at the woman sitting with her knees together in the visitor's chair.

"Disconcerting, eh? Good word, that—I'd use it in a headline if I could. But it's too damn long, for one thing, and for another, I'm afraid ninety-five percent of the people who read the *Journal* would not know what it meant. I'd give five-to-one on that, my girl."

"But it's up to us to educate them, Mr. Hearst."

"You think so, do you? Well, we'll discuss that another time. I've brought you here for an important reason, Weatherall. Bear with me as I ask you a few very necessary questions. All right with you?"

"Would I have a choice, Mr. Hearst?"

"Certainly not. So hear me out."

For a long moment, William Randolph Hearst, the publisher, and Lois Weatherall, the newspaperman—*woman* was not a title as yet—matched surveys. Weatherall stared back at Mr. Hearst, unflinchingly. In the instant, Hearst could readily see that all assessments of Miss Weatherall's beauty had not been exaggerated. If anything, all the fancy descriptions had not done the woman justice. Lois Weatherall was indeed lovely. An American Beauty rose.

Charles Dana Gibson, a leading illustrator of the day, had made famous with his art the sort of woman intended to represent a typical society woman. But through his repeated sketches in all the magazines extant, Gibson had composed a dream girl desired by all—someone that all women would like to have looked like, also. In his pen-and-ink drawings, the artist had fashioned a poised, intelligent-looking, outdoor-type woman who was yet every inch the soft, shapely, feminine Eve. With an upswept pile of hair adorning an exquisite face of wide, appealing eyes, a heart-shaped mouth, and a nose of cameo perfection; in white shirtwaist, with billowing sleeves and ankle-length skirt and hats wide-brimmed and soft-brimmed: the Gibson Girl was an ideal. Lois Weatherall was all of her, and more. Much more. Her eyes had almost violet hues in them; her mouth was a pursed marvel, as though ready for a kiss. The long dark lashes of her eyes fluttered in startling contrast to the sheer cream of her complexion and the altogether splendid line of her jaw and cheek. All in all, a feminine creature to turn heads in passing. As it always had. Lois Weatherall, clearly, might have posed for the Gibson Girl who graced the pages of *Harper's* and *Scribner's* and all the other periodicals. In the living flesh, it was she herself who was disconcerting. Added to which, her voice had an innate softness and delicacy that was completely in rhyme with her appearance. And totally alluring.

Seated now in the upholstered straight-backed chair just across from the massive desk behind which sat enthroned America's most famous newspaper publisher since Horace Greeley, Lois Weatherall, in white shirtwaist and full skirt, her raven-black tresses en bouffant to frame her magnificent head and face, waited.

The Hearst office was high-ceilinged and thickly carpeted, with tall casement windows overlooking the avenue. The walls were paneled in dark brown wood and boasted more framed documents and certificates of awards and the like than one might find in an archive center. The photographs of Mr. Hearst posing with famous people were beyond count, too. Lois Weatherall tried not to look impressed, but she was. Mr. Hearst had had his picture taken with kings, queens, and all the greats and near-greats of the sports world and the theatre. Lois recognized P.T. Barnum, John L. Sullivan, Jenny Lind, Grover Cleveland, and Queen Victoria of England. There was even a picture of Mr. Hearst with General Tom Thumb, the smallest man in the world. Mr. Hearst was obviously much younger then—not the sallow-faced, prematurely aging young man who was eyeing her so very speculatively at this very moment.

The owl eyes were shrewd, though. Very shrewd.

Visible proof of the lively brain and keen mind behind the eyes.

William Randolph Hearst had earned every bit of his reputation.

"Now then, Miss Weatherall, how much am I paying you a week?"

"Twenty dollars, Mr. Hearst."

"I see. And whose department, may I ask, is graced by your presence?"

"I'm with Mr. Rogers. The Society Page. Mr. T. Rogers."

"And what do you do in Mr. T. Rogers' department?"

"Copy-editing, mainly. Of course, every now and then Mr. Rogers permits me to write up some of the announcements. You know—marriages, anniversaries, tea parties, luncheon meetings—"

Suddenly, the owl eyes bored back at her. The nasal voice rose in a challenge. "Sounds infernally dull. However necessary. Tell me—is that what you want for a career, Weatherall? Writing social squibs?"

Lois Weatherall's impeccable chin tilted. The violet-shaded eyes flashed with something. Something vital and sensitive.

"No, Mr. Hearst. I do not."

"What do you want, Weatherall?"

"I want to write the news. I want a byline. It isn't something only men can do, you know. I think Nellie Bly proved that for all time when she sailed from Now York around the world to beat Phineas Fogg's record in Verne's *Around The World In Eighty Days*—"

Bemused, Hearst cut her off with a laugh and a broad wave of both arms. "Please don't educate me, Miss Weatherall. I am well aware of Nellie's exploit. *The World* had one of the newspaper stories of the century with that exclusive—'' Joe Pulitzer had beat him to the punch with that one, but in all fairness, it was before his leadership of the *Examiner*, turned over to him by his father; that had been *The San Francisco Examiner* and Hearst had made it a success before buying *The New York Journal* in '95—when Lois Weatherall must have been a child, judging by the young, innocent look of her. ''Tell me, my dear. How old are you?''

One never did ask a lady her age unless that lady worked for one. Lois Weatherall sensed the distinction and smiled unconcernedly.

''I shall be twenty-two my next birthday. October twenty-seven. But really, Mr. Hearst, I'm wise for my years—''

''Are you now? That's interesting. I have a great need for a woman wiser than her years. Where did you go to school?''

''Hunter College, here in New York. Though I hail from Pittsburgh, originally. My folks were schoolteachers—American history and geography—''

The owl eyes twinkled with softness.

''Ah—a city child. Splendid. That is what is called for on this assignment. A city child. I can't mess about with some frail country flower who will faint at the first drop of blood—are your parents content that you are working on a newspaper in big, wicked New York City? Tell me the truth now—it's most important.''

The violet eyes clouded. Lois Weatherall shifted in the big chair, ever so slightly and delicately. "They are both dead, Mr. Hearst. I lost them no more than a year ago. That awful train wreck in Canton, Ohio. They were on their way to a Civil War reunion. Dad had been a drummer boy with Grant's army at the Wilderness. He enlisted as a very young boy—I imagine that's why he taught American history. He was so in love with this country. And Mother, well, she could name the remotest spot on the map in all the world. They were quite a pair, my father and mother. I loved them very, very much."

William Randolph Hearst harrumphed in a low tone. Genuine sentiment and humility always made him uncomfortable. Miss Weatherall had told him all this with a gentle and proud air of sadness. For an undecided moment, Hearst weighed the woman he was seeing and hearing against the project he had in mind. The project won. He placed his hand on the desk and stared closely across the desk at Lois Weatherall.

"Do you want to hear what your assignment is, Weatherall?"

"You know I do, Mr. Hearst."

"Very well then. As you may or may not know, Richard Harding Davis is on his way to Cuba to cover the war for this newspaper. He is unquestionably the finest man in America for the job. Do you agree?"

"Oh, absolutely. His copy is brilliant. I've read most of his material and all the stories—it's peculiar that we've never met. He's come into this building many a time but I've never caught a glimpse of him once—"

"I don't doubt that at all," Hearst cut in sourly. "Had he ever set eyes on you, I'm sure he would have mentioned it to me. Dick Davis is not blind and he does have an eye for the ladies. But let that pass for a moment—does the name Brian Dexter Cook mean anything to you? Tall young man, very blonde hair, eyes bluer than the Northern Lights, and more tan than an Aztec Indian."

Lois Weatherall frowned. The effect was altogether charming.

"I can't say that I have. Should I know who he is?"

"Perhaps, perhaps not. In any case, he is your assignment."

"I beg your pardon?"

William Randolph Hearst smiled in almost a fatherly fashion.

"The Society Page has blunted your wits, Miss Weatherall, else you would know that Brian Dexter Cook is the finest and most promising newspaperman to come down the pike since Dick Davis. Also, he is—or was—a byliner for this newspaper, dear. A young man who only a day or two ago told me to keep my millions and find myself a new boy. He's jumped ship on me, and my spies have informed me he's gone over to the enemy camp and may be working for Mr. James Gordon Bennett on this Cuban thing. Are you following me, Miss Weatherall?''

''No.'' The frown widened, accompanied by a shake of the lovely head. ''I can't say that I do—''

''Then I shall elucidate and clarify my meaning. I believe in insurance, all kinds of insurance. Dick Davis will be my man in Cuba. But I want someone there with him, should anything happen to him. A war is a hazardous thing, Weatherall. Something could happen to Davis. I want Cook there with him to back him up, as it were. You see what I mean, I think. Richard Harding Davis is the best in our business. I think Brian Dexter Cook has the makings of a Davis. Therefore, I want him there, too—in Cuba. Now do you understand?''

''No, I do not. If Mr. Cook doesn't want to work for you, how can I—a total stranger—have any influence over him at all?''

Hearst permitted himself a smile. A knowing smile. He leaned back in his own upholstered leather chair, more ornate than the one Lois Weatherall occupied, and regarded her very carefully.

''Hear me out, girl. And listen well. I know what I am talking about. I am an expert in these matters. I know Brian Dexter Cook—I know his temperament, his goals, the way he sees this world of ours. I am telling you he is a hopeless romantic, a knight of the old school, the sort of man I didn't think existed anymore. He weeps for mankind, God bless him, and he will do anything for a deserving woman. I think you can be the one to talk him into joining Dick Davis in Cuba as a staff member of my *Journal*. He'll work again for me if Miss Lois Weatherall convinces him that is what he ought to do. And should do. You understand my meaning now, I think?''

Lois Weatherall shook her head uncomprehendingly.

''Really, Mr. Hearst. Just what is it you are asking me to do?''

Hearst lost his poise. He leaned forward and pounded a heavy hand on the massive desk. ''Good God, woman! Haven't you listened to me? Brian Dexter Cook will carry your scarf into battle if you asked him to! He'll do anything you ask, if only you have the power and the will to make him fall in love with you! Must I draw a diagram for you, Weatherall? I'm employing you as an agent—a secret agent, if you will—to make one of my prize rabbits come back home. Use your head, woman. You are easily the most beautiful thing I have seen in New York in years, and by the Almighty, if you can't turn an impressionable young Don Quixote's head, then nobody on God's green earth can, and that's *a fact*. Now don't talk for a moment. Don't get righteous or goody-goody on me. Sit there and think over my proposition. It ought to be a pleasant enough task—Cook is as handsome as a man can be. And you will have carte blanche. All expenses paid; the sky's the limit. And at the end of the road, if you are successful, there will be a column waiting for you. A byline column in the *Journal*'ll make you more famous than Nellie Bly, whether you can write well or not. Think, Lois Weatherall, think. I'm offering you fame and fortune.''

Lois Weatherall gasped.

A ladylike gasp.

What Mr. Hearst was suggesting was unthinkable—unconscionable—why, he was asking her to be a hussy, a vixen, one of those scarlet women who lead men down the primrose path, solely with her guile, her feminine charm—her *body* . . . why, it was Delilah all over again! And Carmen and Circe and . . . Mr. Hearst was asking her to be unscrupulous! The thought was staggering. For long seconds, her lips were locked, her mind rioting, her determination to succeed shaken.

''Well?'' William Randolph Hearst snapped regally. ''What is it to be? The Society Page forever or the birth of a bold, enterprising young woman who could turn out to be a very famous reporter?''

The loaded query hung like the sword of Damocles in the high-ceilinged office. The atmosphere was suddenly charged more with tension than with Mr. Thomas Edison's electricity.

Lois Weatherall set her lovely chin.

''What is it you wish me to do, Mr. Hearst?''

The great publisher sat back in his ornate chair, his shoulders relaxed. His big face was satisfied, content.

He was an expert at judging people and he was happy he had not erred in his evaluation of the truly beautiful young woman seated across from him in his office, the place where he made so many important, crucial decisions for the *Journal* and his people.

"You'll know what to do, Miss Weatherall," he said quietly, "when the time comes. But first you shall have to meet the gentleman, won't you? Toward that end I have a sheet of information here which will tell you all you need to know about him: where he is staying in town, what his habits are, his likes and dislikes. Also a photograph of Mr. Brian Dexter Cook—"

Lois Weatherall nodded, all too quickly, trying very hard not to feel as if she had just made a bargain with some kind of devil.

Or the very Devil himself.

Mr. William Randolph Hearst was just a trifle frightening.

The way he did things!

Whatever his motives were.

Or might be.

## FIFTH AVENUE AND FIDDLESTICKS

Miss Lois Balfour received Mr. Brian Dexter Cook that sunny, eventful day in what the liveried butler called the drawing room of the huge pile of masonry and wealth on the corner of Seventy-Second Street and Fifth Avenue. The monied and sophisticated of New York had seen fit to build on either side of vast, green Central Park. Fabulous Fifth Avenue was the place to be seen wheeling about in your carriage and cab. Nothing else would do as a setting for those who had been born with a silver spoon in their mouths—or had garnered one through shrewd business acumen and exploitation á là the Astors, the Vanderbilts, the Rockefellers, and the Carnegies. So Waldo Friedlinger, surely one of New York's Four Hundred—it was claimed that there were only four hundred people in the town's society who were worth knowing or meant anything in the scheme of things—was comfortably "fixed" in the richer environs. Merely a carriage ride away from the most fashionable shops, restaurants, hotels, the midtown theatrical district, and the true heart of the city. Central Park East was an address to envy. Governor Frank Sweet Black lived 'there, too. Let the lower East Side with its low-rent tenements accommodate the numberless immigrants from the European shore. The upper East Side was for those of taste and privilege. The Statue of Liberty, which promised equal opportunity for all, was still but a symbol of hope and a bright future. It had not exactly paid off on that promise as yet.

The Friedlinger drawing room was a large, glistening affair arranged in blonde wood, with parquet floor, a book-filled glass cabinet in one corner, and four matching settees with ottomans to complete a setting of tasteful luxury. There was a spinet cater-cornered to casement windows that looked out on the sunny avenue. The drapes, tucked back to allow the sunlight to enter, were pure velveteen, richly hued. And then there was Miss Belfour, a fine picture of grace and beauty, rising to greet him as he entered the room. The silent butler had vanished somewhere. Discreetly, soundlessly. Brian Dexter Cook took Linda Balfour's hand and bowed ever so slightly. He admired luxury such as this, though he had no desire ever to accumulate the sort of funds that could afford such surroundings. He was too young as yet to be corrupted by the idea of a large, personal fortune. But he appreciated the setting—yea, verily.

"It's ever so nice of you to come."

"I think I would have been an idiot not to."

"Oh."

"May I sit down?"

"How silly of me—mustn't forget my manners—do sit, please."

Seen in broad daylight, freed from the garish lights of Delmonico's, Miss Balfour was even more attractive than he had remembered. The oval face was as palely beautiful as a Spanish woman's, ever eternally shaded from the sun in those walled gardens. Her features were all delicate, too: the eyes small, the nose slight, the mouth a rosebud. The dark hair was arranged around the oval in a coiffure most becoming. Miss Balfour's figure was Dresden-doll-like, altogether fetching in a green lace dress whose bodice and full skirt seemed to touch off all of her best points. Brian Dexter Cook, neatly arrayed in a brown woolen suit and as golden and healthily glowing as ever, studied her soberly. The damsel in distress of the night before was clearly a lady to the manor born.

"This room is lovely, Linda."

"Yes, isn't it? I've always liked it—" Linda Balfour suddenly seemed ill-at-ease. She spread out her dress with her slender hands and cleared her throat. "Well, here we are again. I do want to thank you for last night. It could have been an ugly scene."

He shook his head. "I'm sorry I had to hit Uncle Waldo."

"I'm afraid he deserved it. He does drink too much—oh, can I offer you anything? We have a well-stocked liquor cabinet. I don't touch it myself, but perhaps . . ."

"Thank you, no." He smiled. "When I'm in the company of a beautiful woman, I never feel the need for spirits."

"You mustn't say things like that, Brian."

"Why mustn't I?"

"Because I like to hear them, but they seem simply small talk. And you're probably just saying it because you think I like to hear such things. As all women do."

He laughed easily, not unkindly, enjoying her company and his own lighthearted mood. Hearst, his assignment for Bennett, Cuba, and the sailing next week all could wait. This was *now*.

"I shall tell you, then, something you have never heard before."

She peered almost shyly from where she sat on one of the settees. "And what is that may I ask?"

"Your name. *Linda*. It is the Spanish word for beautiful."

"Oh," she said, again pleased immeasurably. "And how do you know that, Mr. Brian Dexter Cook?"

"I took a Spanish primer from the office, knowing this Cuban business was going to take a lot of my time soon enough. I'm brushing up on the language. It should come in handy."

"It has already." She smiled. "And you are right. I never have heard that before. *Linda*—now I like my name more than ever."

"It's a beautiful name," he agreed softly. "For a beautiful young lady."

Linda Balfour collected herself. "You are a rake, aren't you? As well as Sir Galahad. I see I shall have to watch myself in your company. You could turn a girl's head, saying such pretty things. Be warned. I like you already, but I'm not about to hand my feelings over to someone who is going to rush off to some nasty war."

"I'm not rushing off." he protested.

"May the seventh," she reminded him. "You told me on the telephone. And I don't believe in war, for any reason. I'm with Uncle Waldo on that. We have no real business or right to interfere with the Spanish. After all, what concern is it of ours that they're having troubles running their country—''

"Remember the *Maine*," he said abruptly, harshly, feeling a flash of genuine anger that was not quite right, certainly out of place in this fine room with this fine-looking feminine creature.

"Fiddlesticks," she snapped back, showing fight. "We still aren't sure how that happened, are we? And everyone knows how your Mr. Hearst and the other newspapers stirred the whole country up."

"He's not my Mr. Hearst. He's nobody's man but his own."

"You say. It's really a shame how he's used that unfortunate incident to sell newspapers. I'm a librarian, Brian. And I do read. I'm not just one of your silly, feather-headed females who don't know what's going on in the world—''

"I'm glad to hear that," he said coldly, trying to contain himself. The lovely scene was getting out of hand. He could feel it. Suddenly, the afternoon that had promised to be a lark of some kind was taking on drastic nuances. He rallied. "Look, Linda. Let's forget about politics, wars, Mr. Hearst. All right? The most important thing right now is the two of us. I don't want to spend the day discussing the problems of the world—''

"Why?" she challenged, tossing her head. "Do you imagine I'm not capable of having a sensible debate with you on the subject?"

"No, of course not. It's just not my notion of a pleasant way to spend our time—surely, you agree?"

"I do not. I think it's a good way to spend our time. After all, between a man and a woman, there must be other things besides—besides—" As straightforward and determined as she was, she faltered. And Brian Dexter Cook seized the advantage and the opening.

"Fiddlesticks?" he suggested teasingly.

A bright red spot appeared in each of her alabaster cheeks.

She turned her face away, but too late.

Again, he seized the moment. He rose quickly from his chair, crossed to where she sat, and stared down at her. She had to turn back to him, sensing his nearness. She looked upward almost fearfully. He saw the pulse quickening in her ivory throat, the sudden rise of the well-shaped breasts pushing against the green bodice.

She saw clearly now what other women saw when they looked at Brian Dexter Cook.

There was something unique about the compact six feet of him. The broad shoulders, the fine-featured face, the deep blue eyes, the unbridled golden thatch of hair cresting the bronzed mask. When he smiled, the effect was altogether appealing and magnetic, somehow. She had never seen whiter teeth. She felt her knees trembling.

"Don't you dare try to kiss me—" she said in a small voice.

"Why shouldn't I try?" he murmured, lowering himself.

"Because ladies do not allow that on first meetings—"

"But this is our second encounter. Remember? I met you last night in Delmonico's."

"You also struck my uncle. A dear relative of mine."

"He deserved that. And you said so."

"I have changed my mind. Uncle was right to tell you what he did. You and Richard Harding Davis. You're both going to make a game of this horrible war—"

"Will you please stop talking nonsense? They sunk the *Maine*; we have to take a stand, have to help those rebels in Cuba—the government is tyrannical—we're Americans—it's our duty—"

"Innocent people will be killed. They always are. The women and the children and civilians. I know my history, Brian. I know war. It isn't right—nothing can make it right—"

"Dammit," he blurted, "stop that kind of talk right now—" He reached down, took her two frail wrists, and drew her full-length to him. She could not resist. For a moment, their eyes locked—his angry and icy blue, hers brown and fearful. Then he crushed her to him, planting his mouth firmly down on her rosebud lips. She tried to cry out but couldn't. The kiss sealed her. For one long moment, she surrendered, melting to him, returning the kiss. And then her sense of the rightness and fitness of things, of time and place, returned to her, and she pulled away from him, trembling. He let her go, recognizing defeat. He did not dodge or duck, either, as her outraged arm drew back and delivered a resounding slap flush across his face. Ladies, in 1898, simply did not allow gentlemen to take liberties on such short notice. Particularly in their own homes.

The hard blow stung, but Brian Dexter Cook did not reach up to assuage the pain. He merely nodded and stepped back.

Linda Balfour cringed on the settee, recoiling as though he were some monster in one of those plays currently attracting theater-goers on Broadway and Times Square. Mr. Clyde Fitch and Miss Minnie Maddern Fiske could have played this scene in any of their modern high-society plays. Beau Brummell and Becky Sharp.

"How dare you—" Miss Linda Balfour gasped.

"I'm a newspaperman," Brain Dexter Cook said simply, not without pride. "We have to dare all things."

"I'm afraid I'll have to ask you to leave. When I invited you here for lunch, I never dreamed—"

"Don't be a hypocrite, Linda Balfour. You certainly did dream. You're a librarian and a woman.

And they dream all the time. That's why they read books so much—''

"Get out," she begged dramatically, burying the oval face in two feverish hands. "I never want to see you again. Not ever, Brian Dexter Cook— you're a beast!"

He waited only a second longer, then sighing, marched very quietly toward the door through which he had come. She began to sob on the settee, not really sure of her own feelings or motives, not knowing whether she really wanted him to go or not. The moment was so deliciously different, so out-of-the-ordinary, so intimate. It was a scene to remember, and she was savoring every moment of it, no matter how upset she was. As for Cook, he was truly disappointed. He had envisioned a far different kind of afternoon for himself and this ravishing young society wench. To have her transform into simply another conniving, rather abrasive female was a bit too much for his romantic soul. The game was not worth the candle, as Mr. Arthur Conan Doyle liked to have Sherlock Holmes say. Dan Quixote was upset with a Dulcinea who had gone against the script by behaving like a schoolgirl.

Brian Dexter Cook reached the door, turned the ornamental knob.

Linda Balfour heard the noise and unearthed her weeping, oval face from her hands. She could not believe he was *really* going.

"Don't you have anything to say to me?" she wailed. "After your disgusting, ungentlemanly behavior, Brian Dexter Cook?"

His smile was extraordinarily handsome from the depths of the doorway. "Ah, but I certainly have, Miss Linda Balfour."

"Well—I'm waiting for your apology—it's the least you can do, isn't it?"

"Fiddlesticks, Miss Balfour," Brian Dexter Cook said very coldly. "Fiddlesticks."

And slammed the door in departure. Without apology.

Miss Balfour collapsed on the settee in a sobbing, wailing heap.

Brian Dexter Cook no longer cared.

His principles, his code of behavior, his ideals, all had probably cost him a grand lunch in a rich house, and the company of a beautiful heiress with very possibly even greater rewards and pleasures at the end of the day—but he did not care.

There is a price no man will pay for a woman. Any woman.

With Brian Dexter Cook, it was righteousness.

Not even soft lips and warm flesh would ever cause him to play the hypocrite to win the spoils. Or ever say what he did not mean.

Damn, but it could be a lonely road sometimes, feeling the way he did. Still, he was whistling cheerfully as he descended the stone stoop that fronted Waldo Friedlinger's mansion, ignoring the man on duty there. The sun was in the heavens and all was still right with the world, to paraphrase Mr. Robert Browning, that fine English poet.

Even if God was not in his heaven over Cuba and Manila Bay where Dewey waited with his six ships for the American Army to come—ships which had not suffered a single scratch in the Manila Bay engagement that had made George Dewey America's Man of the Hour.

Mr. Cook was no longer reprising "My Wild Irish Rose."

As he strolled up sunny Fifth Avenue, rather enjoying his new-found freedom, passersby noted that the tall, handsome young man was rendering a pretty good version of "Columbia, the Gem of the Ocean." John Philip Sousa, the legendary band-master of the United States Marine Band, the March King, would have applauded. Brian Dexter Cook had a fine baritone voice and a very faithful ear.

Thus, Brian Dexter Cook on the afternoon of May second in 1898.

A day when momentous things were happening, when enterprises of great pitch and moment, to quote William Shakespeare, were in the offing. The Spanish-American War had put all America on the alert.

America and many, many people, individual and otherwise.

A war that would change many, many lives.

\*     \*     \*

Richard Harding Davis, bags packed and head and heart set for the Cuban assignment for William Randolph Hearst and the *New York Journal*, was having his last drink in the bar at the Hotel St. Regis before setting out for the night train that would take him to Florida before he caught a boat to Cuba. It would be the fastest and most comfortable way to get to the battle zone in Havana. Davis had been all around the world before, covering Europe and Africa in his dispatches; he had reported Queen Victoria's Diamond Jubilee in London, England, but this would be his very first sample of real-life danger. A war. Brian Dexter Cook had said something about leaving by boat for Havana, but that was too slow for Richard Harding Davis. He was spoiling for action and excitement. It was one of the qualities that had made him such a famous correspondent. And now Cuba—and a genuine war. There had been no more time to say good-bye to Brian, but Brian knew how he felt. He had wished his young friend good luck with the James Gordon Bennett job and let it go at that. William Randolph Hearst needed no more defense from Dick Davis.

"Render up to Caesar that which is Caesar's," the Bible said. Well, Hearst was certainly a king among newspaper publishers.

As he paid up his final bar tab in the St. Regis, he spotted Stephen Crane again, idling in the vestibule studying a handsome reproduction of the *Mona Lisa* by da Vinci. This large canvas in oils hung

near the cloak room where all could see it on their
way to the bar. Davis decided that young Crane
looked as morose as ever. Unbidden, he remembered how Crane's phenomenal success with his
Civil War novel had led to stories of the use of
drugs. And then had come the chronic stomach
trouble which had plagued the young author since
his coverage of the Greece-Turkey turmoil for Hearst
in '97. But Davis had come to his defense long
ago by stating "as soon as Mr. Crane's success
began there were ugly stories set in circulation
about his private life."

Despite their vast differences in style, the way
they saw life and so many other things, Dick
Davis liked and admired Crane. *The Red Badge of
Courage* alone spoke volumes for him.

Crane saw him coming and smiled wanly, drawing his eye away from the *Mona Lisa*. "Hello,
Dick. Getting ready to shove off for Willie Hearst?
The word's out in every drinking establishment in
town."

Davis smiled. "Just about. And you—how did
you fare with the Navy examination?"

"Not sure about that yet. They are either in no
hurry to enlist naval officers for this thing or I'm
just not up to snuff. At any rate, Joe Pulitzer is
sounding me out about covering Cuba for *The
World*."

"Splendid." Davis was genuinely pleased. "Fact
is, I was telling an admirer of yours only yesterday

how well-equipped you'd be for the assignment. Brian Dexter Cook. I did want to arrange an introduction for him—he did want to meet you—but I'm afraid I'll be long gone by that time, Steve.''

"Cook?" echoed Crane, frowning. "Where have I heard that name before? Sounds very familiar."

"I think not. You were in Greece and London while he was making a bit of a name for himself with the *Journal*. He's written a series of fine pieces for Hearst. The kind that roots up facts, points the finger at shady dealings, and generally makes City Hall and the crooked politicians tremble."

"Oh. And what is he doing now with all this Cuba business going on? Staying behind to watch the home fires?"

Dick Davis shook his head, his eyes a trifle sad.

"Far from it. He's walked out on Hearst and signed on with the *Herald*. He is a young man of principle, it seems. A mite foolish, but altogether an admirable fellow. You'd like him."

"I'm sure I would." Stephen Crane smiled warmly. "Where can I find him before he leaves town?"

"The Algonquin, I think. He should be there another week or so. If you do look him up, please mention my name."

"That I shall. Well, good luck, Dick. Come back all in one piece. And beware of knives—the

Spanish are great believers in the knife as a form of execution. Personal and political.''

Richard Harding Davis shook hands warmly with Stephen Crane.

''Duly noted, Stephen. And the best to you with the Navy and everything else. God take care of you.''

''Thanks, Dick. The same to you.''

They parted, these two disparate men whose only common bond was their love of the written word. And the reporting of battle and what it does to human beings. But Davis admired heroism and gallantry. Stephen Crane always questioned the wisdom and sanity of it all. He saw beyond the medals, the flags flying, the patriotism.

Yet in each of their hearts was the mutual love for America and all things American. Old Glory was no mere piece of fabric to them, no adornment solely for schoolhouse walls and parade grounds.

The phrase *war correspondent* was about to take on a richer, fuller meaning because of men like Davis and Crane.

And Brian Dexter Cook.

In far-off Washington, D.C., under a peaceful blue sky dominated by a warm sun, the Capitol dome thrust upward like a monolith on the monumental horizon. Within its polished corridors, the lawmakers and executives of the nation were busily setting in motion the machinery of the mighty government known as the United States of America. And in no single office, no solitary room, was activity more concentrated or organized than in the large, high room that housed Congress. The members were in a fever pitch of excitement this day. Great happenings were in the offing. What the nation did next in the matter of the Spanish-American War was the very uppermost item on the agenda.

And the personal decisions of certain executives were also to have their far-reaching effects. Like a pebble dropped into water.

Consider the conclusion to which Theodore Roosevelt, Assistant Secretary of the Navy, had at last come to. Irrevocably.

He had made up his mind, this ebullient, hale and hearty, outgoing man, who had been so critical of the President's slowness to act in the matter of Cuba prior to the sinking of the *USS Maine*. The outspoken man had said of President McKinley: "He is a white-livered cur." And perhaps, even more critical than that: "He has prepared two messages, one for war and one for peace, and doesn't know which one to send in!" The newspapers, William Randolph Hearst, and mostly Theodore Roosevelt had been urging McKinley to declare war on Spain as soon as the *Maine* went down in Havana Harbor. When McKinley at last conceded that war was the only solution to the dilemma, Roosevelt hardly softened his criticism.

In truth, his ultimate gesture of defiance was the one he was about to enact now.

On this day in May. With America rolling up its sleeves all the way. With the entire nation in a frenzy of patriotic fervor.

"Mr. President, there is something that will not wait. That I must discuss with you."

"What is that, Mr. Roosevelt?"

"I should like to tender you my resignation as Assistant Secretary of the Navy."

"But now is not the time for such a move. I need you here. The nation needs you—"

"Mr. President, I will be much more useful elsewhere. For months now, since this unrest in Cuba began, I have been writing all my old friends in the Dakota territory. The cowboys, the wranglers, the men who know horses. Horses will be useful in this Cuban campaign, believe me. And these men—all are old, good friends—will be willing to come as volunteers. To ride with me in the Cuban campaign as part of the cavalry regiment we intend to call the First United States Volunteer Cavalry. I estimate a force of about one thousand men who will all be good shots and good riders. My word on that, Mr. President. Leonard Wood will command when the regiment is formed. I must be free to assist him. I will be needed in putting the outfit together. Such a unit would be incalculably valuable to the Army, Mr. President, as a striking force, as reconnaissance scouts, as trouble-shooters in tight spots.''

"Wood is a good man, Mr. Roosevelt. But I wish you would stay on here. The Administration—"

"Can do without a trouble-maker such as myself.'' Theodore Roosevelt flashed the toothy, bespectacled smile that had already won him thousands of admirers and adulators across the country. "Come, sir. Be honest with me. I am a thorn you would be glad to remove from your hide. The Party has had a bellyful of my complaints and arguments. They'll all be glad to see me go. Some may wish I never come back from Cuba.''

President William McKinley sighed. "I never could win any arguments with you, Mr. Roosevelt. Very well. I accept your resignation as Assistant Secretary of the Navy. I'll make the official announcement today, if you like.''

"Bully, Mr. McKinley. Bully!''

Whenever Theodore Roosevelt was enthusiastic or approving, *bully* was the word he always used. It might have been his battle cry. It was the word all America was to come to know him by, identify him with, and affectionately remember him by.

Teddy and T.R., as he was generally known, was already of the stuff and caliber that American heroes are made of—something that William McKinley, in his wisdom, might have noted.

In any case, no matter the conditions, Theodore

Roosevelt was no man for anyone to have as an enemy. He was far too formidable.

And in this way and on this day, the Rough Riders were rather unofficially born—a regiment with a date with History.

It was born in William McKinley's presidential office on a fateful day in May. And an out-going Assistant Secretary of the Navy marched jubilantly from the President's presence, his rimless glasses twinkling, as he rubbed the palms of both hands together in nearly juvenile excitement and happiness.

Theodore Roosevelt was already the father of five children at the age of forty—Theodore, Jr. (1887), Kermit (1889), Ethel Carow (1891), Archibald Bulloch (1894), and Quentin (1897)—but he had all the spring and zest and panache of a much younger man. He was the Boy Eternal. Something William McKinley was not and never could be. But Fate had intertwined their lives inexorably.

And there was no turning back now.

Destiny was on the move once more.

An assassin's bullet on September 6, 1901, would fell William McKinley, a scant six months after his second inauguration—a sad day at the opening ceremonies of the Pan-American Exposition in Buffalo, New York; a tragedy that would make Vice President Theodore Roosevelt, at age forty-two, the youngest man ever to assume that highest of offices. But neither Teddy Roosevelt nor William McKinley were aware of such a calamity that day when T.R. took his leave of the President of the United States of America.

It was still only 1898.

And the Spanish-American War was yet to be fought.

To the finish.

Whatever that might be.


Uncle Waldo Friedlinger came home from his fashionable club in the middle Fifties later that afternoon to find his favorite niece dry-eyed and seeming out-of-sorts, sitting by the big windows that looked out on Fifth Avenue. The child had never lookd lovelier—she was so like her mother Cecily—but Waldo Friedlinger knew his niece all too well. So he put aside his own personal inner rage at the newspaper accounts he had read of his fall from grace at Delmonico's—the boys at the club had been sympathetic and understanding, knowing how newspaper devils distorted the facts—and thumped up to Linda, putting on an air of cheerful good health.

"What's this, girl? Moping on such a lovely day?"

"Oh—hello, Uncle." Her tone was like dead ashes.

Waldo Friedlinger frowned and stalked to the liquor cabinet to mix himself a refreshing drink. His florid face was always softer whenever he was in the company of Linda Balfour. She was tonic for him.

"Blast it, child. Something's up. I know you too well. Tell your old Uncle, eh? Maybe I can help."

Linda Balfour sighed. A maidenly sigh. Her dark eyes brightened. But only for a fleeting moment. "Uncle."

"Yes, child?"

"When did you know you loved Aunt Susan?"

Uncle Waldo blinked, his cocktail glass frozen in one beefy hand. "That is a very curious question, child. Your blessed aunt has been dead over twelve years now and—" He paused, perplexed. "Love? Humph. Well, it simply happens, that's all. A feeling comes over you. From out of the blue, you might say. And there you are. I really cannot think of a better way to explain it, dear."

"Is that the way it was with you and Aunt Susan?"

"Well—yes—she was stunning, you know. Everyone thought so. We made a handsome couple back then—I was the envy of many a man. Yes—quite." Uncle Waldo Friedlinger's eyes suddenly took on the mist of warm memories. He shook himself. "Blast you, young lady! What in the name of Time is this all about?"

Linda Balfour turned her back to the windows.

"Nothing, Uncle. I just wanted to know how it

was. I have never been in love before. Not ever. I
want to be prepared for it when it does happen . . .''

"Prepared?" Uncle Waldo Friedlinger threw back
his head and laughed. Not unkindly. "Why, bless
you, child. You haven't heard a word I have said."

"I beg your pardon?" She had turned her eyes
to him again, surprised. The oval face was nearly
startled.

"Linda, Linda. I told you. It comes at you from
out of the blue. Just like that." Uncle Waldo
snapped his fingers. "Prepared? Not on your
tintype. It simply happens. Take my word for it."

"Oh," Linda Balfour murmured, remembering
broad shoulders, blue eyes, white teeth, and a
molten, flaming kiss which had left her temporarily stunned, until she had behaved like a silly idiot
in a romantic novel. Her heartbeat quickened. She
smiled.

"Uncle Waldo, you're an old bear, but you're a
dear."

"Am I, indeed?" Her uncle sipped his scotch
and soda water. "Our stockholders will be amazed
to hear that. They rather fancy me an ogre who
refuses to share the profits with them."

"Just the same. A dear."

"If you say so, child."

That marked the end of the discussion. Uncle
Waldo had no more to say on the subject of love.
But for Linda Balfour, the rest of the day was a

charming, soaring voyage of self-discovery—heady and dizzying, and also a little frightening, somehow.

Can a woman truly fall in love with a young man she has hardly seen for longer than half an hour? An *almost* stranger?

Miss Linda Balfour did not know.

And therein lay the wonder of the whole affair.

And the magic.

Spring in New York had claimed another victim.

Albeit a very willing one. The Balfour heiress-to-be.

Young men might have the fancies, but it was the women who had the dreams. Fantasies and yearnings. Wishful forget-me-nots.

Dreams from which there was no turning back.

Miss Lois Weatherall, she of the Gibsonian face and figure, was busy making plans in her private room at Mrs. Lanigan's Boarding House on West Eighty-Second Street. Here, amidst mansions and rich homes just off Central Park West, there were still rooms to be had for young, single females who worked for a living. Lois Weatherall had found Mrs. Lanigan's domicile, a mere block from the Museum of Natural History, on the corner of Columbus Avenue and Eighty-Second, a true home away from home. Mrs. Lanigan was corned-beef-and-cabbage Irish; the linen was always clean, and an air of Christian charity and sweetness dominated the environs. There was no drinking on the

premises; gentleman callers would be greeted in
the parlor, and if you could play the pianoforte, as
Mrs. Lanigan could and often did, why, you were
welcome to that, too, dearie. Lois Weatherall liked
Mrs. Lanigan. The broad, burly woman who had
come to America because of the Irish potato fam-
ine way back when was now a widow because
Patrick Joseph Lanigan, her late husband, had been
crushed under the wheels of a beer wagon during a
raging storm downtown on Union Square. Her
children, Patrick Joseph, Jr., and Nancy Mary had
both married and gone off to their own lives.
Patrick was a streetcar conductor in the Bronx and
Nancy a housewife in Canarsie, Brooklyn, married
to a plumber. Mrs. Lanigan was eminently cheerful and good-natured, for all of that. And she had
never lost her love of Ireland or her hatred of the
rich who lived so well while millions all about
them lived so poorly. *It was not God's doing!*

Lois Weatherall had always found her a tower
of common sense, decency, and kindness. In many
ways she reminded her of Norma Brown Weatherall,
the loving mother she had lost too soon.

It was within this comfort and safety that Lois
Weatherall mapped out her campaign against Mr.
Brian Dexter Cook. Mr. Hearst and the staff had
provided her with a wealth of information and
material relating to the rising young newspaperman.
A trove, indeed.

There were sheafs of clippings saved from the

files, the columns and stories written by Brian Dexter Cook. There was a form that was filled out with his complete personal history, right up to the first day of his employment on the *Journal*. So Lois Weatherall learned all about Mr. Cook and his background. He had been raised on Statan Island, graduated *cum laude* from Cornell University, and had entered the Hearst world with a personal letter of recommendation from the dean of Cornell—a letter to Mr. Hearst himself from an old friend. Yes, the details were all there for her—including the report on the death of Brian Dexter Cook's father and mother in the collapse of the bridge in the Bronx: this hit Lois Weatherall like a hammer blow to the senses. To think that both she and Brian Dexter Cook were orphans—members of that fraternity and sorority that were far too large in the country of the late eighteen-nineties. Roger Williams Cook, ferryman, and Emily Plank Cook, lithographer. How strange—her own father and mother—American history and geography. Schoolteachers. That awful train wreck—

At that moment in the silence of her room, with dusk coming on and the shades of evening compelling her to turn up the gaslight, Lois Weatherall felt a unique kinship and softness for this young man she had not met, the one William Randolph Hearst was asking her to dupe. For a long moment, she fought with her inner convictions and beliefs. And then her slender fingers plucked the photograph of Brian Dexter Cook from the top of the thick, rubber-banded file once more. She had only casually glanced at it at first, so eager had she been for the facts about her prey. Now she studied the photograph and could not quite explain or understand the subtle sense of warmness and pleasure that suddenly stole over her. Her breath almost caught—her fingers trembled ever so slightly.

The photograph was obviously a replica of Brian Dexter Cook's college graduation sitting. There was the black mortarboard, the calm, stoic face, unsmiling. But she could see the chiseled perfection of his features, the strength in his jaw, and the wild blond hair bursting from beneath the mortar board. The expression in the clear, direct eyes was all too uncommon. This photograph of him, coupled with the really fine articles he had written and that she had already digested, words and ideas that said something, that stamped a good, sympathetic mind—all this combined to produce in her a feeling of anxiety and expectation. She wanted to meet Brian Dexter Cook now. Truly meet him and talk to him and see if the man of real life was the man in the college photograph. Pictures did lie sometimes.

She could hear the pianoforte playing downstairs. Mrs. Lanigan, probably. The old woman always liked to play something while supper was on the boil in her steaming kitchen. She had a house full of hungry boarders and Mrs. Lanigan never let them down. Her meals were absolutely nourishing and wholesome. Tasty, too.

Miss Lois Weatherall put aside the Hearst morgue material and paused to listen. The silvery notes were wafting up the narrow stairwell as they always did. Almost a signal that suppertime was close at hand. Music soothed the savage beast—at least until he was fed! Lois smiled at the random thought. And the image.

*. . . just a song at twilight*
*when the lights are low*
*and the flickering shadows*
*softly come and go. . . .*

What a lovely song. So tender and gentle and loving.

So peaceful, so nocturnal, so sad.

Lois Weatherall sighed anew.

How *was* she going to meet Brian Dexter Cook?

This romantic young man whose preferences were Alexandre Dumas, James Fenimore Cooper, and Whitman, Twain—and *Knights Of The Round Table, Ivanhoe, The Three Musketeers*; this young man who wrote so idealistically of the people and working conditions and damsels in distress—surely, Don Quixote and D'Artagnan were his *beau ideals*!

*Damsels in distress.*

Miss Lois Weatherall smiled. A woman's knowing smile.

It had come to her. The idea, the scheme, the plan.

Now she knew how to encounter Brian Dexter Cook.

Of course. It was perfect. Like a made-to-order dress.

Mr. Cook was doomed. His fate was sealed. Mr. Hearst would be proud of her. She was going to hoist Mr. Cook on his own petard.

He would be trapped by that which his whole life, background of interests and heart, soul and mind would not ever let him ignore.

How in the world could Mr. Brian Dexter Cook resist a damsel in distress? A gentlewoman sorely in need of his assistance?

He would not; he could not.

And therein lay Miss Lois Weatherall's master plan.

An hour later—with the piano stilled and supper on the table, with Mrs. Lanigan clamoring up the stairwell and throughout the house for all to "Come and get it!"—Lois Weatherall tripped happily down the carpeted stairs, singing under her breath. She was content.

It would all be so pricelessly simple.

When you thought about it.

Rather like leading a thirsty horse to water.


Nearly two thousand miles away, churning up the blue-green waters of the Caribbean Sea, the North Atlantic Squadron under Rear Admiral William T. Sampson had already begun its partial blockade of Cuba. Sampson's fleet, tactically, had been on a search for the Spanish fleet which had left Spain guided by Admiral Pascual Cervera y Topete, that veteran commander. But now, with radio signals constantly keeping him in touch with Dewey and the amazing feat-of-arms, the talk of the fo'castles and mess rooms, the entire U.S. complement was ready for further battle. Sampson had wired his congratulations to Dewey, and now Cuba was in a veritable pincer-squeeze with America's Asiatic Squadron to its north and the North Atlantic Squadron to its south—a very strategic and effective boxing of Spanish forces. Cuba was in a very precarious vise of American might.

From the bridge of his flagship, Rear Admiral Sampson surveyed the desolated vast expanse of waters before him. His squadron was splayed out behind him, covering his flanks for miles in either direction. But there was no sign yet of Cervera and his ships. The sky overhead was leaden and grey. There was no sun.

Far, far off to the east, the Spanish fleet flitted and stole ghostily for the landlocked harbor of Santiago. A phantom force. Admiral Pascual Cervera y Topete was eluding Sampson's squadron with all the cunning and seamanship at his command. Spain could not afford to suffer another Manila Bay so soon. There was still time to rally, regroup, and strike when the moment was right. Santiago could yet save the humiliating situation Havana was dealing with—total blockade, while the *Ameri-canos* waited for their precious army to come.

But as far as the Spanish were concerned, there was only thing awaiting American forces that tried to land on Cuban soil. One supreme, inevitable outcome.

*Muerte por los Americanos!*
Death to the Americans!

# STATEN ISLAND AND SERENADE

In New York Bay, about five miles from the long strip of land known as Manhattan, lies Staten Island. Ferries had ever linked the two islands. There was simply no other way of reaching shore on either side, unless, of course, one had one's own sailing vessel or had the wings of an angel or could fly like the birds. Since no resident of either island could lay claim to such phenomena, everyone took the ferry to and fro. The fare was but a nickel and the ride itself a pure delight. From the bounding depths of upper New York Bay, beginning at Battery Park, the southernmost tip of Manhattan Island, the ride began. The view en route was scenic and eye-filling. Ferryboat passengers saw Ellis Island of immigration fame, Bedloe's Island with the spectacular Statue of Liberty rising up from the water like a stone goddess. Staten Island was known as the Borough of Richmond, but nearly every New Yorker thought of it as Staten Island.

And the seagoing trip itself featured close-up views of Brooklyn and the rising Palisades of New Jersey. The Hudson River fed into New York Bay, ending the long stretch of waterway on which Hendrik Hudson had sailed his *Half-Moon* so very long ago. All in all, a kingly trip, and all for five cents—the nickel coin with the V mark on one side and the Liberty head on the other.

The day following his falling-out with Miss Lois Weatherall, Brian Dexter Cook decided to take the ferry from Battery Park out to the island. Nostalgia as well as necessity had dictated the journey. For his passage to Cuba on the good ship *Marlboro*, he would require his steamer trunk and telescope, a Bausch and Lomb dandy—these two valuable leftovers from his days at Cornell were bound to come in handy for the Bennett-*Herald* assignment. He hadn't wanted to keep them on hand at his hotel where they could be easily stolen. Instead, he had kept them in safe storage at his parents' old bank on Staten Island. Now he could repossess them because he needed them, and also he could revisit the spot where he'd spent such a happy, carefree childhood. Memory of Roger Williams Cook and Emily Plank Cook would be evergreen for Brian Dexter Cook.

When he quit his hotel room that morning to find a carriage in front of the Algonquin, he was surprised to see that it had rained earlier in the morning. A wet sidewalk and dampened cobbles greeted him. This did not dampen his enthusiasm, however.

Light of heart and expectant, he hailed a carriage and in no time at all was clattering downtown to Battery Park. He could have taken a trolley car, but the longer ride and many stops at street corners would have delayed and bored him. Besides, horse-drawn rides appealed to his sense of court-liness.

He never saw the closed hansom cab that fell in behind his own transportation. Nor could he have seen the breathtakingly beautiful woman ensconced inside, a woman who had waited nearly an hour for him to emerge from his room. She had planned in advance and planned well, learning from the polite clerk at the downstairs desk that Mr. Cook always appeared in the hotel lobby around the hour of eight before leaving for the offices of the *New York Journal*. But, of course, the beautiful lady knew that Mr. Cook would not be going to the

*Journal* this day. He no longer worked for Mr. Hearst and the *Journal*. He had resigned. Quit.

As the two leather-enclosed carriages clip-clopped down Broadway, heading for lower Manhattan, the tall buildings of New York seemed dark and forbidding in the thin mist that lay over the stone canyons of the city. But a suggestion of breaking light parting the massed clouds above suggested that the weather would improve. There was a fine, brisk feel to the air. The wind would sweep the lingering raindrops away, surely, as it always did.

It did. Finally, most beautifully.

A pale sun broke through to warm the landscape.

By the time the carriages wheeled into Battery Park, no more than thirty yards apart, the day bade fair to be a fine one.

Old Sol was out in force now, beaming brightly.

On the choppy waters of the bay, the huge, squat ferryboat easing into the slip, accompanying its arrival with regulated blasts of its horn, was a welcome sight to all the people standing in line awaiting its arrival: Men, women, children, and a bevy of Italian-speaking immigrants eager to see the Statue of Liberty once again—the Lady with the Torch who had been their very first sight of America the Beautiful, the Land of Opportunity, the Land of the Free and the Home of the Brave. *Veramente! Una buona signora!*

Brian Dexter Cook, newspaperman that he

was, understood the spectacle and reveled in it. These were the tools of writing: the people, the places, the things—all the emotions and events.

The lovely creature in the cab behind him did not alight from her vehicle until Cook had already joined the patiently waiting line on the dock. Then, and then only, did she climb from the rear, pay the driver, and walk gracefully to the slip's edge. The horses whinnied.

The gathering sunlight seemed to sparkle off her picture hat, blue sailor's jacket, and full-length flowing white skirt. Her fine athletic stride and sure movements bespoke of poise and intelligence of a high order. She glittered in full sail, trim and seaworthy.

No woman ever drawn by Charles Dana Gibson ever looked more beautiful. She would have glorified the cover of any magazine.

Brian Dexter Cook saw her not at all.

He was too busy moving forward, sidestepping debarking passengers and hurrying to find a solitary place for himself at ship's rail. He had much to think about and he wanted to be alone.

Miss Lois Weatherall hastened in her pursuit of him.

She wasn't going to let him get away.

Not this man—in spite of Mr. Hearst's assignment, Brian Dexter Cook, the man, interested her more than a little.

A very great deal, in fact.

He looked like a man worth *knowing*.

For more reasons that one.

The plan came to realization before the mammoth ferryboat with its shipful of passengers reached the Staten Island side of the bay. Lois Weatherall had to work fast before she lost her determination and her nerve. After all, if she was going to provide Brian Dexter Cook with a damsel in distress, it had better be the real thing. The genuine article. Not some mere matter of his making like a gentleman, no. He had to have the opportunity to act like a hero.

The opportunity came soon enough. And Lois Weatherall, if she was anything at all, was spirited and resourceful.

Once she found Brian Dexter Cook—at the rear of the broad vessel, posed at the railing, staring somberly at the receding Manhattan shoreline, seemingly lost in the gushing wake of the big ship which broiled up the bubbling waters of the bay—she made her move.

He was as tall and handsome as ever, his golden thatch of blond hair billowing in the breeze, and there were very few people within his immediate vicinity. Only a middle-aged fat woman in peasant skirt whose hands were full of children, several eager, tousled-haired youngsters gawking at the sights of the harbor. Lois Weatherall, now no more than fifteen feet from Brian Dexter Cook, leaned dangerously over the wooden railing and waited for the slipstream to catch her wide, unattached picture hat. The huge paddle wheels would have to be avoided at all costs, but Miss Weatherall knew what she was doing. In reality, she could swim like a fish—something Mr. Cook would not be aware of, certainly. And if he was any kind of gentleman at all . . .

She took a deep breath, let the wind take the wide-brimmed hat and flutter it out to sea. She blurted "Oh, dear!" loud enough to be heard by anyone within a distance of fifty feet and desperately flung her arms and body out as if to catch the runaway chapeau.

That, in effect, accomplished all she had hoped for.

And everyone standing in the stern of the good ferry *Richmond* saw what happened next. And could only gape on in shock, fear, and utter paralysis of movement. It all happened too quickly, too fatally.

The beautiful young woman in the blue sailor's jacket and full-length skirt pitched over the long railing, falling outward before she could catch her balance. She had reached out too far for the errant hat and in her misjudgment toppled over the railing, losing her equilibrium and her safety. Lois Weatherall shrieked, crying out in desperation and terror. Everyone heard the pitiful shout, the supplication for help. And assistance of any kind. *Someone had fallen overboard!*

The falling woman struck the heaving waters like a rock which has fallen from a great height. In fact, the distance from stern rail to the surface of the bay was no more than fifteen feet. But it was enough.

Lois Weatherall disappeared beneath the surging waters.

Brian Dexter Cook did not have to think twice. If he thought at all.

He had not seen the woman, did not know who had fallen overboard, but it seemed not to matter. The wailing, shouting cries of the children with the fat, middle-aged woman yet rang in his ears as he rapidly kicked off his shoes, athletically mounted the rail, arched his arms, and swan-dived into the bay, cleaving the waters like a knife. The *Richmond* foghorn blasted; a ship's bell clanged shrilly. Passengers came running, exclaiming, jabbering excitedly. Tragedy had struck and reaction was total and fearful. *Dear God, that poor young woman* . . .

On board, someone with good sense, possibly the pilot, stopped the churning paddle wheels of the *Richmond*. The broad, squat, seagoing leviathan chugged to a slow, cumbersome halt. All the passengers had now flocked to the starboard side of the vessel, straining their eyes at the spot where the lady, and then the gentleman who had dived in after her, had gone down.

Governor's Island lay behind the *Richmond*, and within sight was the fabulous Statue of Liberty dominating the shore before all the onlookers. A tense, sudden, deathly silence gripped the throng.

And when two heads suddenly, magically reappeared, breaking upward from the troubled surface of the waters, the man holding on to the limp figure of the woman, a mighty cheer went up. A thunderous roar of relief, pleasure, wonder. People began to applaud and whistle and shout their joy as Brian Dexter Cook stroked magnificently toward the halted ferry, his other arm locked about Lois Weatherall's shapely form. She had, in fact, gotten more than she had bargained for.

Great swimmer that she was, not only had she not reckoned on the water's near-freezing temperature, but the full-length skirt and her silly high-button shoes had become dead weights on immediate contact with the water. Her miscalculation had almost cost her her life.

Damsel in distress, indeed.

Thank the Good Lord for Brian Dexter Cook.

He had been epically heroic. On the grand scale. Truly Homeric.

By God, he was beautiful!

Every soul on the *Richmond* was in unanimous agreement.


The captain of the ferryboat handled the entire situation with nearly loving care. A large, barrel-

chested, red-faced giant named Swenson, he was
also a bit of a romantic himself, not to mention a
salty character who enjoyed the sensation on his
ship that day. After all, a rescue at sea, a lovely
female saved from drowning, all sorts of excitement:
never had the dull voyages of the *Richmond* offered so much to talk about. Captain Swenson was
very equal to the task suddenly placed on his big
shoulders.

Two thoroughly drenched and cold young people,
abruptly helpless and in need of a Good Samaritan.
The young fellow had acted like a prince, *yah*, but
now he needed help, too. As for the young lady—
Captain Olaf Swenson had never seen a more beautiful woman. Not even in long-ago Norway where
pure Scandinavian beauty flourished traditionally.
This American girl was something—*yah, yah*.

So he allowed them to use his private cabin,
equipped them with heavy, coarse blankets, and
made them a piping hot pot of coffee while the
*Richmond* continued on its routine schedule of
back-and-forth for the tourists and the sightseers.
After all, what else could be done? The young
people were not hurt; there was no need for medi-
cine or doctors. Their problem was simply getting
their clothes to dry so they could go ashore without catching their death of cold. That and getting
their chilled blood circulating once more. The drip-
ping wet clothes were hung over the ship's bridge
rail. A few trips across the bay and they would be

dry soon enough, what with the sun and the cool
winds. And so it was done—and Lois Weatherall
and Brian Dexter Cook were left alone in the
captain's cabin, which held a lean-to, thank the
Lord, and all that was left was to wait. After they
undressed, privately.

Freed of the first shipload of well-wishers, back-
slappers, and admiring humans, Brian Dexter Cook
was now wrapped in mountainous blankets. As
was Lois Weatherall. A wooden table separated
them, with each sitting on a bunk across from each
other. There had been little time for little of anything save Lois Weatherall's *Thank you*'s—which
she said repeatedly—and Brian Dexter Cook's
*You're welcome*'s. And when Captain Swenson
left them alone so he could see to his helm and the
return trip to Battery Park, there was a long, awkward silence between them. A charged, suspense-
ful silence in which each hardly knew what to say
or when to say it.

For two very good reasons. Most unusual ones.

Brian Dexter Cook had never seen a more bewitchingly beautiful feminine creature in his life.
Gibson Girl, be hanged. He was not reminded of
the Gibson Girl. Instead, he saw a radiant, violet-
eyed, dark-haired marvel whose every expression
and slightest movement sent curious thrills racing
through his veins. Even with the long dark tresses
damp and clinging, Lois Weatherall was unforgettably beautiful. He forgot Miss Linda Balfour in

the merest of seconds. She might not have ever existed.

As for Lois Weatherall, no, the photograph in Mr. Hearst's file had not lied. But it had been merely the tip of the iceberg. Never had she seen a more glowingly handsome, attractive man. The almost somber face was intimidating, but mainly because the faintest smile showed her his sparkling teeth and those deep blue eyes. Nor could she readily, or ever, forget the comfortable feeling of his powerful arms in the water and how his shoulder had been a bulwark for her as he pulled her to the safety of the life preservers flung overboard by quick-thinking passengers.

Brian Dexter Cook was becoming more than an assignment.

Already he was an adventure.

And when she thought of the true purpose of her being in his company and the lengths to which she had gone to achieve such an end, she could feel a guilty twinge of shame. And doubt.

What would he say if he ever knew or found out that she hadn't fallen overboard accidentally but had deliberately jumped?

"How did you fall in?"

The short query came from him so abruptly, smashing the awkward silence to atoms, that she very nearly started. His voice was so resonant, so richly timbered.

"I lost my hat. The wind blew it off."

"Your hat," he repeated. "And then?"

"I tried to catch the silly thing. I reached out too far over the railing."

"You shouldn't have done that. It was dangerous."

"Yes, it was, wasn't it?"

"You might have drowned."

"I might have. But I didn't, thanks to you. You're a wonderful swimmer. You handled me as if I were a bag of feathers."

He shrugged almost apologetically. His face was bleak now. "Was it a very expensive hat?"

"Oh, no. You can buy hats very cheaply. This one was no more than one dollar and ninety-five cents."

"Then it was a silly thing to do. Very silly."

"I'm sorry. I made you get all wet and probably spoiled your day for you . . ."

"I'm sorry, too. For sounding huffy like I did—" All at once, the brightest and handsomest of smiles illuminated the bronzed face. "It was probably the purest reflex action—you reaching for your hat, I mean. Like a child running after a balloon across railroad tracks. Forgive me—I'm cold and irritable, I'm afraid."

"I don't think you're irritable at all," she said ever so softly. "And after all is said and done, you did save my life. And I'm never going to forget that."

"I wish you would. Any man would have done the same thing in my place."

"But you're the man who did it and that's what counts, Mister—I don't even know my lifesaver's name—"

"Brian. Brian Dexter Cook."

"Lois." She smiled. "Lois Weatherall. I'm very pleased to meet you." They did not stand up or reach over to shake hands. That would have meant releasing their holds on the blankets that covered their nakedness. Both seemed to realize this at the same time, and their smiles and sheepish laughter were mutual.

From outside came the blast of the ferry whistle. Brian Dexter Cook stared across the table at Lois Weatherall.

"We're heading back to New York. Then Staten Island again. Look, our clothes should be dry by then. Where were you going today?"

"To see the Statue, of course. From a ship's rail. I never tire of the sight. Not much else. Then I was going back to town. And you?"

"Oh, just a trip back to the past. I was born on Staten Island and I was going to pick up some things there. A telescope and my old steamer trunk from college. You see, I'm leaving the country later this week—in four days, to be exact."

"Oh. How interesting." She pretended not to pry, though she knew darned well what his destination was. "I have never really walked around

Staten Island. And I've the whole day to myself. Would you mind very much if I went with you? After all—'' She smiled the smile that would have melted stone. "We have shared quite an experience already and I do want to know more about you, Mr. Cook.''

"Miss Weatherall—'' he began, not too strongly. "Lois—''

"Yes?''

"I would be delighted, ma'am.''

They went back to their cups of deliciously hot, aromatic coffee almost guiltily, each one very much impressed with the other.

Lois Weatherall knew now that William Randolph Hearst had not exaggerated one iota in his evaluation and description of Brian Dexter Cook. The man was truly a heroic gentleman. Handsome, dashing. Genuinely modest and unassuming.

Brian Dexter Cook knew in that precious moment together in Captain Olaf Swenson's cabin on the *Richmond* that he had met the woman he had secretly yearned to meet all his born days.

The damsel in distress.

The *beautiful* damsel in distress.

Not Ivanhoe, not D'Artagnan, not Sydney Carton had ever had the likes of Miss Lois Weatherall to assist.

Lady Rowena, Constance Bonacieux, and Lucy Manette could not hold a candle to this exquisite woman whom he had plucked from the ocean. This nymph, this paragon, this goddess—

William Randolph Hearst's scheme was under way, in full swing.

Samson had been baited by Delilah.

The rest of the plan was up to Delilah, now.

Miss Lois Weatherall had more than a pair of shears to work with.

Much more.


They had a wonderful day together.

The sort of day that lovers and sweethearts really have but once. When everything is new and all is fresh, exciting, and just a little bit frightening. For to fall in love, to yield to the blandishments and attractions of another soul upon this earth, is perhaps the greatest gamble or risk of any single person's life. There is a great danger in that—for it is a surrender of a sort, as well as a triumph. To give one's self to another is a great gift—and the handling of that gift is the hazard, the danger, the peril of it all.

The cards were stacked against Brian Dexter Cook and Lois Weatherall. They were going to fall in love with each other, no matter what. And it all had begun with an unscheduled dip in upper New York Bay.

When their clothes were dry and they stepped ashore on Staten Island, they were a mite rumpled and wrinkled, but no one would have paid much attention to that. The girl was lovely, the boy handsome, and the new fresh sunlight set them off like diamonds on a velvet cushion in Mr. Tiffany's windows on Fifth Avenue. Captain Olaf Swenson waved good-bye to them from his bridge, all smiles and paternally exact. He felt as if he had sat in on the beginning of a grand romance.

As well he had.

Brian took Lois to his bank in another carriage. There they retrieved the precious telescope and the steamer trunk. The trunk, empty of anything, was not all that heavy, and Brian laughingly remarked that it was just as well Lois was along. She could help him carry the thing. As she did, with one of them at either end of the rather large box. It was not a metal trunk, merely a wicker affair bound in red buckram. Brian called it a "family heirloom." His mother had used it in her own college days. So they handled it carefully and lovingly. Lois was enjoying every minute in this man's company. And when he suggested lunch at a pleasant little tea room no more than a block's walk from the bank, she readily agreed. She had worked up quite an appetite by this time.

Between the two of them, they did more than justice to country sausages, a delicious cheese omelet, deep dish apple pie, and a large pot of coffee. Conversation, however maidenly shy, was no longer guarded or tentative. Brian Dexter Cook had relaxed, and all at once, he was telling her all about himself—the Cornell days, the death of his wonderful father and mother, the *Journal* career. He led right up to the present difficulties with Mr. Hearst and stopped, leaving that hanging. Lois Weatherall could now see that the Cook demeanor, so habitually poker-faced and all too solemn, was a mask to cover an innately sensitive man who kept a lock on his emotions publicly, but who in private was very obviously warm-hearted, outgoing, and terribly friendly. She did not for a moment imagine that it was herself who had worked the transformation. Yet she had. Brian Dexter Cook was all at once the schoolboy, the vulnerable young man, eager to be heard and understood. Like a boy trying so very hard to impress a pretty girl . . .

"The day off, you said," Brian suddenly cut into her thoughts. "And what kind of work do you do in that big city of ours, Lois?"

She didn't want to lie, not just yet, but she had to because he was having such a monumental effect on her own feelings and emotions.

"Oh, you know how it is with women. Men don't think much of us as workers, beyond sewing or waiting behind ribbon counters and such. I'm afraid I'm not much more than that—"

His teeth flashed in a smile.

"That doesn't tell me anything. You're being evasive."

"Am I? I didn't mean to be. I'm only an assistant floorwalker at Gimbel's Department Store."

"Really? I'm impressed. Not many females could rate that unless they were a cut above other women."

"You'll turn my head with sweet talk like that, Brian."

"The truth will out, Miss Weatherall. Remember that. Old newspaper axiom. More coffee?"

"Yes, please."

Staten Island was dreamland now. The atmosphere, the suddenly gorgeous weather, the feeling of sharing—it was all of a piece. By the time they returned to Captain Swenson's ferry for their return trip to the island of Manhattan, the big steamer trunk joining them together somehow, they were both so wrapped up in one another that they were hardly conscious of the time of day. The long telescope rattling about in the interior of the trunk was worth more than one joke. They made a game of its random bouncing about within the buckram sides of the thing. Yet the afternoon was hard on three o'clock, and when the huge ferry slipped into Battery Park, neither one had any idea of quitting the other's company. So Lois accompanied Brian back to the Algonquin where he turned the trunk over to a lobby porter to carry it up to his room, and from that point on, they truly had the day to themselves. Brian Dexter Cook took charge of her. And she let him, knowing full well he had made up his mind and was not to be turned aside or denied. When he took her arm and locked it in his own, they were as one. His touch was exciting now. Even more so than it had been in the freezing waters of the bay. For now it somehow meant even more. Together, they left the hotel, not as each had earlier that day in separate horse-drawn carriages, but walking toward Broadway. It was a day to see the sights and share them. The weather could not have been more ideal and their thoroughly dried clothes no longer were an eyesore. No one would have noticed anyway.

They were in luck.

They caught a parade going up Broadway, the United States Army in full panoply—uniformed men, flags and divisional banners unfurling, cannon and caisson trundling along. Crowds lined the sidewalks, cheering and waving small pennants and caps and hats and bonnets. A huge banner proclaimed: WE'RE ON OUR WAY—CUBA OR BUST. The spirit of the throngs was solidly behind the parading military force, a detachment from the Kingsbridge Armory on the lower East Side. As Brian Dexter Cook explained to Lois Weatherall with a sad, grim smile on his handsome face, he had not wanted to be reminded of the Spanish-American War and his Cuban assignment. Not today, no. Today was for himself and this fantastic creature at his side. He did not want to share her with anyone. Or anything.

So he took her on a tour of the city.

Chinatown, Little Italy, the Jewish ghettoes,

the East River waterfront, the Brooklyn Bridge spanning two boroughs. She saw Union Square, Greenwich Village, Gramercy Park—all on one sweeping tour of Manhattan in a four-wheeled carriage drawn by two proud horses. When she protested that he was spending an awful amount of money on her, he pooh-poohed the thought with: "You are worth every penny, dear lady. And besides, my bosses expect me to live like this. How else can I report things if I don't familiarize myself with the city? Forget it, please. This day is on me. And I couldn't be happier."

"Oh, Brian—"

"Yes?"

"You're going to spoil me."

"My intention exactly. You deserve spoiling—"

"You could turn a girl's head—"

"That, too, is my intention. Didn't you know?"

The afternoon wore on, filled with fresh new sights and the wonderful *now* feeling of wanting to be with somebody, wanting to know someone far better than you even know yourself. And getting the most incredible senations from merely the pressure of a warm hand. Or the flash of a marvelous smile. It was all so amazing, really. She would not have believed it could happen so fast. This thing called—*love*. If that is what it truly was . . .

They had dinner at Luchow's on Fourteenth Street, the popular Viennese restaurant so famed for its dining atmosphere and its cuisine. Brian did not want to take her to Rector's or Tony Pastor's. Luchow's, he somehow felt, was the place to take this woman he had suddenly found in a world full of females, on a windswept morning in upper New York Bay. Somehow, Luchow's seemed right. The candlelit tables, the aura of Old World elegance, the waltzes played by the orchestra—"The Blue Danube," "Tales Of The Vienna Woods," "You and You"—

And then they danced together. And it was done. A *fait accompli*.

The whole incredible go-round since Captain Swenson's ferry came to its inevitable, preordained conclusion. Eros won in the end.

With their arms around each other, there was no longer any denying the thing that had sprung up between them. The feeling; the deep, rapturous, headlong emotion. The once-in-a-lifetime joyous rapture.

With the music at its swirling peak, the violins all pitched to a romantic frenzy, their bodies touching, their eyes meeting and saying so many unspoken things, there was no turning back. No more pretense, no more sham. Neither maidenly or gentlemanly.

It had happened at last.

Brian Dexter Cook and Lois Weatherall had fallen in love.

And it happened somewhere around a quarter after nine on the dance floor at Luchow's Restaurant on the evening of May the third, eighteen hundred and ninety-eight. In the year of the Spanish-American War. During a Strauss waltz known the world over as "The Merry Widow."

For these two very young people, the world was a beautiful place indeed. And it was so wonderful to be alive—

And in love.

All on a purely golden day when the Asiatic Fleet and the North Atlantic Squadron of the United States Navy was closing in on Cuba from the north and the south, all guns trained on the blockaded island.

It was indeed Cuba—Or Bust.

The Stars and Stripes flew gaily from all superstructures.

America, Warrior America, was on the move.

# CENTRAL PARK AND CUPIDITY

The days that followed the Staten Island adventure were a romantic haze, a whirlpool like no other, in which one lost one's self in the eyes and arms of another. Brian Dexter Cook and Lois Weatherall shared their first kiss on the night he took her home from Luchow's to Mrs. Lanigan's boarding house on West Eighty-Second Street, and from that kiss forward, the die was cast. They were in love, hopelessly, romantically, dizzily in love. What was to happen between them now was purely in the lap of the gods, in the hands of Fate.

For Brian it was walking-on-clouds time. He had never been in love before, if one discounted his schoolboy crush on one Miss Theodora Smith, his English teacher, she of the limpid eyes and full red mouth. But that had been unrequited, of course, since Day One.

For Lois, there had never been anything in pants. Career and getting ahead in life had been her end-all and be-all. That is, until now. Until Brian Dexter Cook, darn him.

What was worse, not once had she been able to launch her campaign against him, the one Mr. Hearst had assigned her to do. Get him to forget his ideals and silly notions about journalism and come back to work on the paper. The *Journal* needed him, not Mr. James Gordon Bennett and the *Herald*. But every time she was with Brian, her knees and her resolve melted, and she got lost in the magnetism and wonder of just being with him. Still, time was running out. His boat, the *Marlboro*, was leaving the day after tomorrow, and she was at a loss as to what to do.

Brian took her sightseeing daily, dined her in the best restaurants along Broadway and Madison Avenue. He took her to Central Park for boating on the lake. He walked her through Shakespeare's Gardens and toured her through Yorktown where the German immigrants had set up a miniature homeland for themselves with traditional shops, stores, *brauhauses*, and stage shows in little theatres. Belvedere Castle in Central Park became a place where they picnicked almost daily for three days. And then, with the world about them talking nothing but the Cuban conflict and America's part in it, with them concentrating only on themselves and this wondrous emotion that had sprung up between them, the fatal moment arrived when she had to remember who she was and why she had really taken up with this handsome devil in the very first place.

It happened on the lake in Central Park. Brian had rented a rowboat and was rowing her powerfully and easily about the perimeter of the lovely waters, the Manhattan skyline behind them, the tall stone buildings thrusting upwards like so many monuments to the advance of Civilization and Progress. Lois was trailing one lovely hand in the water, her beautiful face shaded from the sun by an elegant parasol. The white, flowing dress she wore clung to her curved figure delightfully. Brian, in boater and belted blue worsted suit, never looked handsomer.

It was another bright May day. The war seemed an impossible thing. So did newspaper assignments and Mr. Hearst and deadlines.

"Why am I so lucky?" Brian asked suddenly. His grin was impish.

"What do you mean, Brian?"

"Well, I meet you, you meet me, and it's only a week from my sailing for Cuba and it just happens to be your week away from Gimbel's. It's incredible, I say. I can't believe I was so luck—"

"Please," she begged. "Don't remind me. It only makes me know that the day after tomorrow this lovely week will come to an end."

He shook his head vehemently.

"It's not going to end for us, Lois. Not ever. I'll go to Cuba, cover the war—why, it will be over before you can say Jack Robinson. See if I'm not right. And then when I come back . . ."

She stared down at her hand trailing in the water.

"Yes?" she urged.

"We will be married. There. I've said it. I've proposed to you. I didn't think I'd do it like that, but it just popped right out of me." He paused, the oars stilled. "Well, aren't you going to give me your answer, Miss Weatherall? Or are you proposed to at least once a week?"

"Oh, Brian. You know I'm not. It's just—"

"Just so soon?"

She nodded, all too quickly. He laughed.

"Yes, it is. I'm as amazed as you are. But it has happened and there is no turning back. Your kisses have made me positively insane, Miss Weatherall. And I want more of them. And much, much more—"

"Brian, you fool."

"Lois, you wonder."

The rowboat drifted under a concealing branch extending out over the lake. Brian did not wait. He shipped his oars swiftly and reached for her, taking her in his arms hungrily. She could not resist him, nor did she want to. The parasol tilted to screen them from the other shore. Their lips met again, as they had so many times in these last delirious days. And it was always the same. Their blood rushed; their bodies trembled. Contact was ever dangerous now.

"Oh, how I love you," he whispered.

"How?" she murmured happily.

"With all my heart and soul, with everything I've got in me. I never dreamed—yes, I did—but I never believed I could meet someone like you. I thought you were only in books and dreams. And in the long ago past—"

"My knight," she sighed. "My own white knight."

"Always," he pledged. "And forever, Lois Weatherall."

The rowboat drifted some more. Until it suddenly struck a projection along the shoreline and pushed out to the center of the lake again. Brian laughed, released her, and redipped the oars, stroking in a slow, easy rhythm to circle the lake once more. Lois sat up, straightening. She closed the parasol. The sun had gone behind a cloud.

"Brian, we must talk. About you and the sailing. It's important."

"Of course it is. The chance of a lifetime, really. Cuba is the only story in the universe at this moment."

"I know that. But that's what I mean. Wouldn't it be better if you went to Cuba as a reporter for the *Journal* instead of the *Herald*? William Randolph Hearst is ever so much more influential than Bennett. That man will do great things someday— you ought to stay on with him, I think. There's no telling how far you could go with Hearst behind you."

He smiled tolerantly. "I told you how I feel. I don't like Mr. Hearst's methods. He distorts the news to his own ends. Just to sell more newspapers. And that is not my idea of running a paper. It never will be."

She bit her lip. She had known this was not going to be easy. She had fallen in love with a man who had a mind of his own. God bless him. It was no small dilemma she had gotten herself in.

"But Brian—your made your reputation with the *Journal*—you told me yourself about those pieces you wrote that gained you so much notice and attention. Doesn't it look rather bad if you go work for someone else? I mean, if I suddenly became assistant floorwalker at some other department store, wouldn't people think Mr. Gimbel had fired me? Think of it that way, Brian, before you rush into something you might regret some day."

"The only thing I regret is that I didn't meet

you sooner. Which reminds me—you haven't answered my proposal of marriage and will you wait for me? I don't want to go off not knowing the answer to either of those questions, Lois.''

"But about Mr. Hearst—"

"Please forget Mr. Hearst. I want to talk about us.''

"But he's your future, Brian. Our future. I don't want you throwing that away so recklessly—''

His blue eyes suddenly narrowed. ''Well. I must say you're taking this more seriously than I have. Why does it mean so much to you who I work for? My stories will be myself, no matter who sends me to Cuba. And James Gordon Bennett has no small reputation, either, my girl.''

She paused, realizing she had stumbled badly. There was a note of suspicion in his tone now. Or rather mild surprise. But that in itself was dangerous. He might begin to add two and two together.

"Really, Brian, you miss the point entirely. It hasn't to do with Mr. Bennett at all. It's simply that William Randolph Hearst hires the best reporters and you're one of them, and when it gets out that you're no longer with the *Journal*, it's bound to be misunderstood.''

"Not by my friends," he said firmly. "Or those who really know me and what my principles are.''

"Oh, Brian, do grow up. That's schoolboy talk. Principles are one thing. Common sense is another. You should work for Mr. Hearst, not Mr. Bennett.

It is where you started and where you should finish."

His eyes lost their warmth and good humor.

"That is still for me to say, isn't it? Come on, Lois. Let's leave this, shall we? I'm afraid you don't understand newspapers and newspapermen. We're a strange breed, at that. I suppose it is difficult for a woman to understand my decision, looking at the dollars-and-cents side of it. But believe me, Mr. Bennett pays quite well, too, if not as high as William Randolph Hearst."

She sighed and decided to back off the subject. She didn't want to rush him or seem too eager. So she laughed and tossed her head.

"Very well, Mr. Cook. Go to Cuba for Bennett; I still cast my vote for Hearst."

"You haven't got the vote yet," he chided, "though I sincerely hope that day comes real soon. It's highly undemocratic and incredibly un-American, for my money, that women haven't the vote yet."

"Bully for you," Lois chuckled, "as T.R. would say."

"Now there," Brian said grimly, "is a man I'd work for for nothing. They tell me he's resigned as Assistant Secretary of the Navy to join up with some volunteer cavalry outfit that's going over there. I've got to learn more about that."

"You will, I'll wager. There isn't much that slips by you."

"You almost did," he reminded her. "Down to Davy Jones' Locker."

She shuddered, no longer play-acting.

"When I think that if you hadn't jumped in after me—"

"Bosh," he said uneasily. "It was a pleasure, ma'am."

"All the same, I owe you my life."

"Then let me take charge of it from here on out."

"All right."

"Do you mean that?" He moved toward her. Quickly, eagerly.

"Try me and see, Mr. Cook." She tilted her mouth.

They kissed again; center of the lake, be hanged. They were in love and it didn't matter anymore who worked for whom. Not for the precious, fleeting moments, anyway. Love was triumphant.

But the devil has his victories too. And now came one of them. As they drifted, unguided by Brian's rowing, they collided with another row-boat coming from the other direction. The craft carried a middle-aged couple enjoying boating on the lake. Unfortunately, the man, a ruddy-faced, rotuned personage, outfitted in straw hat and striped sailing coat, was the last person Lois Weatherall wanted to meet at that moment. She didn't know the stout woman with him, but she knew the man. Oh, how she knew the man. She tried to hide and shrink behind her parasol, but the damage was done. The boats were abreast of one another, and Brian Dexter Cook was already shaking hands in greeting and commenting on what a small world it truly was.

"Why, Thaddeus—good to see you. Hello, Mrs. Rogers. Enjoying Central Park like the rest of us landlubbers?"

"Gracious, if it isn't Mr. Cook," Mr. T. Rogers of the Society Page of the New York *Journal* exclaimed heartily. "Thought you were off to Cuba for Bennett, son and—why, Lois, what on earth! Didn't know you two knew each other—"

"Hello, Mr. T.R." It was a conceit of Thaddeus Rogers that he had the same initials as Teddy Roosevelt and liked to be addressed that way. But Lois practically whispered the greeting, becoming frantic at what this unlucky encounter might produce in the way of results. "Yes, I know Brian. We met only recently."

Brian Dexter Cook frowned, but it was not the frown of suspicion. His hearty smile was perplexed. "Didn't I say it was a small world? Where do you two know each other from?"

T. Rogers blinked and Mrs. Rogers held out a warm, chubby hand in greeting. Lois quickly interjected, "I went to school with T.R.'s daughter Irma—didn't I, T.R.?"

Thaddeus Rogers nodded. He only knew that Miss Weatherall had been pulled from his department on special orders from William Randolph Hearst, and he had not questioned those orders. Now he sensed all sorts of intrigue, and he was newspaperman enough to pick up his cue and save Lois Weatherall's skin, whatever she might be up to.

"That's a fact, son. Well, enjoy yourselves, children—"

Mrs. Rogers was about to protest that her daughter Irma had never mentioned a Lois Weatherall, but Thaddeus was too quick for her. He waved farewell and rowed off rapidly. Brian Dexter Cook, oars up and out from the water, stared wonderingly at Lois Weatherall.

"You are full of surprises. Imagine you knowing old Thaddeus."

"Not so surprising, seeing as how Irma and I were classmates at Hunter College."

"So you went to Hunter College, too." He shook his head. "More and more surprises. I should have guessed. You speak so well. And you seem to have read a book or two."

"More than that," she admitted, trying to lighten the mood. He had already forgotten the incident and briskly oared the water.

"How about we weigh anchor, my girl? Debark and stroll through this lovely park, pausing only to devour a hot dog or two from one of the merchants of meat that patrol these precincts?"

"That," she sighed with mammoth relief,

"sounds perfectly marvelous. I am tired from all the rowing I did."

They both laughed at that and the crisis was over.

But all the rest of that sunny afternoon, Lois Weatherall fretted and worried about the incident. Would Brian think it over later and not be satisfied with her explanation? Would he weigh her arguments for working for Hearst alongside the evidence that she knew the man who ran his Society Page section? It was rather too coincidental.

She needn't have worried. Or concerned herself with possibilities.

Brian Dexter Cook only had eyes for her beauty and a mind set on kissing her at every opportunity that presented itself. Which were many. He seemed to know every nook and cranny, every hidden bench in the park. It was a lovely, thrilling afternoon. Without further snags.

Even though they didn't run into a single vendor of hot dogs.

When you're in love, food is not uppermost in your thoughts.

How could it be?

But Lois Weatherall thanked her lucky stars that she had remembered that Thaddeus Rogers had a daughter Irma about her own age.

And that Mr. Rogers was a quick thinker, too. She had counted on that. William Randolph Hearst did not hire men who were slow-witted.

He always recognized brains and talent and resourcefulness.

Another good reason why Brian Dexter Cook should cover Cuba for the *Journal*. And not the *Herald*.

How was she going to make this young man of hers change his mind?

That was the real problem.

She was truly stuck for a solution.

Yet she was sure one would come to her soon.

It had to. It just had to.

No matter what it cost her in the anguish of her own deceit of a man she not only had come to love but to genuinely admire.

Brian Dexter Cook was one man in a million.


Disaster struck that evening.

In the unlikeliest of all places: Mrs. Lanigan's parlor in the pleasant boarding house on Eighty-Second Street, around the corner from the Museum of Natural History. And once again Lois Weatherall was reminded of the cruel aptness of Sir Walter Scott's Scottish wisdom: "Oh, what a tangled web we weave when first we practice to deceive . . ."

Never did it seem more fitting than that evening when she and Brian were sitting alone in the parlor after supper. Mrs. Lanigan heartily approved of Miss Lois' young gentleman and liked having him about. So Brian and Lois lingered in the parlor; they were tinkling the ivory keys of the old pianoforte. For Lois it was a lovely interlude. Brian could play the instrument by ear and was fingering a reasonable rendition of "Because," currently America's most popular tune and another song made famous by Miss Lillian Russell.

The parlor was clean, tidy, and quite comfortable, what with its deep chairs, long oval hand-woven rug, and clean yellow walls which held most of the things Mrs. Lanigan believed in: portraits of her late husband and two fine children in filigree frames, the flag of the United States of America, and old-fashioned tapestries from the Old Country with embroidered homilies such as "There's No Place Like Home," "God Is With Us All If We Keep Him In Our Hearts," and "Love Thy Neighbor," the Golden Rule of the Bible.

"Oh, Brian, don't you love this room?"

"I do. But I take it you don't care for my playing."

"But I do—honest, I do—"

"Then, quiet please, as I draw toward the finish."

She laughed lightly, happily, as he dexterously closed the piece with a thump on the bass keys. Turning on the stool, he smiled at her almost wistfully. He still counted himself among the luckiest of men. She blew him a soft kiss off the palm of her hand.

It was then, that precise moment, that Mrs. Lanigan came bounding into the room, her wide skirts rustling and her round, cherubic, freckled face flushed with excitement. She was a large woman, formidable and imposing, her graying blonde hair worn in a bundle atop her head. But the magazine she was waving as though it were a fan was the center of attention just then. She was tugging it like a railroad brakeman flagging down a runaway train. Brian and Lois looked at her in surprise.

"It's here, dearie! The newest *Journal*! The one with your fine article in it! I'm ever so proud—I didn't open it until after supper and I near jumped out of my chair—"

Lois Weatherall could have died on the spot, cheerfully.

For a moment, her heart stopped beating, and her tongue stalled in her mouth. Brian, half smiling, looking from Mrs. Lanigan to Lois, was obviously perplexed. "Article . . ." he echoed. "There must be some mistake—I have never submitted anything of mine to the magazines."

Mrs. Lanigan's eyebrows arched in good-natured scorn. She poked a long forefinger at Brian Dexter Cook.

"You ain't the only one has a way with words, Mr. Cook—Miss Lois happens to be a pretty fair hand with the writing language herself."

Swiftly, silently, Brian Dexter Cook took the May issue of the *Ladies' Home Journal* from Mrs. Lanigan's outstretched hand.

He read rapidly, seeing all he had to see and know, and then just as silently, just as wordlessly, turned to Lois Weatherall and proffered her the magazine. His handsome face was set in somber lines once more and the blue eyes had never looked upon her so coldly. So awfully—he looked so . . . *hostile*.

"So," he said without inflection. "Miss Lois Weatherall, Society Department of the *New York Journal*, on the subject of why corsets are no longer necessary for females . . ."

"Brian, I—" She did not know what to say. Not with Mrs. Lanigan hovering like a good-natured ghost. "Mrs. Lanigan—would you please excuse us for a few minutes? There is something I must tell Mr. Cook. Privately, you understand."

The old Irishwoman was nobody's fool. A measuring glance at both these young people had been enough. Something was in the wind. Sighing, she gathered herself together and marched to the parted sliding doors. She had to say something, however, before she left them.

"Whatever it is, or may be, don't fight, darlin's. There's more to life and a man and a woman than words printed on magazine paper."

With that parting sally, she was gone, gone more quietly than she had come, but they could hear her slippered feet padding away.

Lois Weatherall had long since forgotten the offending article. She had sold it to the *Ladies'*

Home Journal months ago. It had been a triumph then. A real break for her career and possible advancement in the echelons of Mr. Hearst's kingdom. Even old T. Rogers had been as proud as a peacock for her. But now it was like ashes in her mouth. The tall, handsome young man standing in the center of the parlor, looking like Judgment Day, was suddenly far more important to her than any article which had paid her the princely sum of one hundred dollars.

With Mrs. Lanigan gone, Brian Dexter Cook broke the hard silence between them. His air and demeanor was decidedly unfriendly, masking the deep hurt she knew he was feeling. A man like him—so honest, so trustworthy, so incapable of deception himself.

"So," he said again, this time mockingly. "It seems you aren't an assistant floorwalker at Gimbel's Department Store. Or did you lose your job with Mr. Hearst just lately?"

"Brian, please. You must let me explain."

"Oh, I'll let you explain, all right. Explain to me why you lied to me, why you come to me under false colors—I should have guessed today when Thaddeus Rogers recognized you. Old Thaddeus is hardly the social type—and all that persuasion you've used on me about going back to work for Hearst—my God, I can't believe I was so dense!" His blue eyes suddenly flamed. "Staten

Island—the ferry—you had to have arranged that, too, so you could fool me completely—''

"Darling, you've a right to be angry, I know. But you mustn't think the worst of me. It was all for your own good—''

He wasn't listening to her anymore. Not really.

"And falling off the ferry—'' He glared at her. "Did you fall in or jump in knowing I'd go after you? Certainly—that's it, of course! A woman who lies about what she does for a living, who really is a reporter herself—'' He broke off, shaking his head in awe of her. "Tell me. Do you seduce men weekly for William Randolph Hearst or is this only the first time? And how far would you have gone—how far?—would you have put your body down for me if I had asked, solely to get me back on Willie's payroll?''

She was so stunned at the accusation she could not speak. What was worse, infinitely worse, was that he had stepped into her, seized her wrists, and roughly pulled her to her feet. Then he released her and placed both hands on her bosom, something he would never have done a moment ago when he thought she was as pure as the driven snow and not a fallen angel. She fell back, shocked, her mouth an oval of amazement and hurt. He didn't care and threw his head back, laughing harshly. Lois turned her face away from him, the tears coming to her eyes. Her bosom scalded where he had touched her.

"Oh, come now, Miss Weatherall," he jeered. "Surely, men have done much more to you than a simple touch? I've minded my manners fairly well, I think. Considering the caliber of woman you are. Why, the dance hall girls and the hussies downtown are more honest than you are, Lois Weatherall. They are what they are and no bones about it. They aren't liars and cheats and hypocrites—"

His voice broke, almost on a sob of anguish and torment. He was a man standing in the middle of a beautiful dream crumbling all about him. And he was fighting back, not as a man, but as a small, hurt boy. For herself, she was incapable of speech or any kind of defense at all. The spectacle of Brian Dexter Cook behaving and acting like a bully and brute was too much for her to comprehend just then.

"Don't tell me you love me, either! I wouldn't believe you now if God came down from heaven. It would be more of your lies, your play-acting—" He moved to the door, his shoes punishing the floor. "And one thing more—tell dear Mr. Hearst his plan didn't work. I'm going to Cuba as planned. For the *Herald*. And I'll thank you never to cross my path again—you won, you Jezebel! You made me fall in love with you—you can tell your boss that—perhaps you'll both get some amusement out of it."

She heard no more cruel, damaging words. He

was gone—fairly stalking through the parted sliding doors. His footsteps thundered.

There was nothing for her to do but collapse on the sofa, her lithe figure spread out in rumpled defeat, her face buried in her hands. His vocal assault, his physical transformation, had been so sudden and savage that it had caught her totally unprepared.

Now she did the only thing that was left to do.

She sobbed, the whole sad business overwhelming her.

Brian Dexter Cook was gone. Perhaps forever.

The only man she had ever loved.

Even if only for a brief time . . . *damn him, damn him!*

After all, what was there to say and do now that all had come to this sad and terrible end?

She somehow knew it was an end. She could feel it in her bones.

She had lost him. She was certain of that.

He was not only going to Cuba for the *Herald*—he was going out of her life. Exit Mr. Brian Dexter Cook. White Knight. Idealist.

Lois Weatherall's low, heartfelt sobbing echoed faintly in Mrs. Lanigan's cheery parlor in the house on West Eighty-Second Street.

She sounded like a little girl.

# TIMES SQUARE AND TAKING OFF

In his tiny, unadorned room at the Hotel Algonquin, Brian Dexter Cook was packing for Cuba and his assignment for the *Herald*. Never had his surroundings seemed more miserable and alien. It was the night before his sailing on the *Marlboro* from Pier 96 and the day after the bad scene in Mrs. Lanigan's parlor. But Brian was trying not to think about that. It had been the first crushing experience of his lifetime—with women, that is. Nothing that ever happened to him in this life would never surmount the tragedy that had taken his two beloved parents from him in the collapse of that bridge in the Bronx. But this was different, somehow. This was a woman—a very special woman—one he had taken to overwhelmingly and rapturously, and now she was like some bad dream. Unreal, artificial, and worst of all—intentionally fake and *bogus*.

He still couldn't believe it; he didn't want to believe it, but the facts were all there. That ravishing female had been set upon him by Hearst for the sole purpose of making him change his mind, alter his course, and go against his own grain. It was the principle of the thing. Lois had lied from the very beginning. And therefore, perhaps, the falling in love was a lie, too. No matter what she said or did now—blast her. He could not get the violet-shaded eyes and lovely mouth out of his head. He had tried the night before when he had stormed out of the house on Eighty-Second Street by drifting into a shabby bar on Columbus Avenue, finding a private booth, and drowning himself in a bottle of Napoleon brandy. But it had not worked. Not even the blandishments of a tired and worn, gaudily dressed lady of the evening who had sat down with him, uninvited, had helped. He had hardly noticed her, or cared, despite her rather pointed attempts to spark some interest in him to earn her money—stroking his thigh very suggestively under the concealment of the round table, then placing her hot hand on his crotch. Brian had not responded. Finally, when she had quit in weary resignation and a toss of her shoulder, and said, guttural-voiced: "Some other time, eh, sport?"—he had nodded, without looking at her, and thrust some paper money at her. He did not see her at all and did not remember her face hours later. She was a drunken blur.

Somehow, he arrived back at his hotel, lurched up the carpeted stairs to his room, and passed out on the bed. When he awoke very late into the next day, his head throbbed and his tongue felt like a lizard in his mouth, and his mind was a battlefield of confusion, doubt, shame, and vast disappointment. He felt as though his whole world had fallen about him. Miss Lois Weatherall had taken over the territory of his being.

But he would not go back; he would not apologize for the things he had said and had done. She deserved his scorn, not his love.

In that ugly mood, he packed for Cuba.

Poignancy and memory assailed him as he stuffed the large steamer trunk with his underwear, his three suits, shirts, ties, and collars. A picture image of Staten Island with Lois at one end of the thing, laughing, her lustrous hair framing her exquisite face—the sound of her voice in that tea room—and then Chinatown, Luchow's, those dreamy waltzes, that first kiss—the touch of her

. . . and then his own hands rudely pressing against her full bosom . . .

Grimly, he slammed the lid of the trunk, blotting it all out in a rush. Then he went downstairs to the lobby to see about some food. His stomach was gnawing at him, restless. He strode into the dining room, found a table for himself, and ordered scrambled eggs, toast, and a pot of coffee. His mood was foul, his face betraying none of his emotions. He was as granite-faced handsome as ever—A trifle worn about the eyes and mouth, but not so much that anyone would have noticed.

It was about three in the afternoon and the room was fairly deserted, most people having already gone about their business. Brian was grateful for that. People were the last thing he needed now. He had to be alone with his gloom, his morbidity, his unhappiness. Like every man before him, ever since the Garden of Eden, he was almost reveling in the betrayal of Lois Weatherall. Now he truly had something to cry about, brood about. Damn all females everywhere!

The Spanish-American War now seemed very remote, indeed. And the names of Dewey, Roosevelt, McKinley and the *Maine* all collided and joined in his head. The faint throb of his hangover disturbed his thought processes. Yes, food would help—give his body something to do. He simply could not think straight anymore.

He had wolfed down the eggs and was on his

third cup of very black coffee, staring straight ahead of him at the far wall with its rather baroque flower-patterned design when an unfamiliar voice spoke just to his right.

"Brian Dexter Cook?"

Standing before him was a youngish man in a rumpled white suit, hair not too groomed, staring down, smiling. Brian nodded and extended his right hand even before the words came: "I'm Stephen Crane. Dick Davis said we ought to get together. They told me out at the desk you were in here."

For Brian, at that moment, he was a godsend.

"Sit down—this is a real pleasure, Mr. Crane—"

"Steve, Brian. No formality between devils who use ink. I hear you're off to Cuba for the *Herald*. Fine paper, that. Used to work for them until I ran into an editor who didn't understand my prose descriptions. May I have some of that coffee?"

"By all means—would you like something to eat?"

Stephen Crane shook his head ruefully.

"Wish I could. The dysentery I picked up in Athens sort of prohibits tasty foods, so—"

"So," Brian Dexter murmured. He had always been impressed with Stephen Crane. It wasn't just that wonderful book he had written—it was the simple fact that this man, despite his youth, was familiar with such famous people as Joseph Conrad,

James M. Barrie, Hamlin Garland, Anthony Hope—the writer of *The Prisoner of Zenda*, one of Brian's very favorite novels. He hardly knew what to say now.

Crane poured himself some coffee. His movements were methodical.

"I admire what you did to Willie Hearst, Brian. Takes gumption to do a thing like that. Not many people would."

"Dick Davis told you, then. It wasn't exactly common gossip."

"Dick Davis told me. Word travels fast in the newspaper world. It's a wonder any sheet ever scoops another." Crane smiled wanly. "Dick thinks a lot of you, Brian. That was testimonial enough for me. So I decided to see you before you go. When do you leave?"

"Tomorrow. The *Marlboro*. Takes me down to Jacksonville. From there I'll arrange something to Cuba, depending on the blockade, of course."

"That sounds about right. I took the trip myself last year when the Turkey-Greece business was brewing."

"And you, Steve? You must be covering this thing, of course—though Dick said something about you wanting to sign on with the Navy or some such—"

Stephen Crane winced. "The Navy is playing me like a virgin female. They haven't committed themselves yet. Either way, I've a standing firm offer from Joe Pulitzer. The *World* needs a man down there."

"Virgin female . . ." Brian Dexter Cook echoed the words, almost subconsciously. Then he shook himself. "You'll be superb covering this war. I mean that. I read *Red Badge* at least three times at Cornell. We all admired it greatly. You know college boys. The fact that a very young man wrote a great book pleased us no end."

His companion frowned. For a moment, Brian thought he had committed a faux pas of some kind. But he hadn't. Crane's next words convinced him of that. "Oh-oh. Do I detect the forlorn lover in that voice somewhere? Or is it simply that the phrase *virgin female* triggers memories for you, lad?"

Brian Dexter Cook smiled sheepishly, then shook himself, going grim again. "I'd rather not talk about it, Steve. Not just yet. Do you mind?"

"Certainly not. But a word of advice?"

"Of course."

"Never let it contaminate your copy. Not ever. The way one female treats a man is not the way of all females."

"Yes—I suppose you're right—but—"

"But it still hurts, eh?"

"Like the very devil." Brian was suddenly very relaxed and in a confidential mood with this writer he admired so much. "Have you got a girl, Steve?"

"I'm a benedict, Brian. I married Miss Cora

Taylor last year and I have not regretted it since. You should be as lucky—"

"Oh, I didn't know."

"Why should you? Cora and I are not exactly Four Hundred types."

They both laughed at that and Brian somehow felt immeasureably better. Nothing had changed, of course. He still had lost the girl, or rather, she had lost him—but at least he could bring her out in the open now, without wincing or hiding about it.

"I want to thank you for looking me up, Stephen Crane. I'll remember this long after it's over. And I do hope our trails cross again. Either in Cuba or back here in the States."

"They will. Count on that. We belong to the same fraternity. Men who have a compulsion to write about things. Or make them up. It's a disease—writing is. And once it is in your blood—" Stephen Crane shrugged and poured himself another cup of black coffee. "Who do you like to read, Brian?" The pale face was suddenly alive, interested.

Brian laughed. "I'm incorrigible when it comes to the storytellers. The romanticists. I grew up on Dumas, Dickens, Fenimore Cooper, Shakespeare—and for the French I'll take Hugo, too—but—we don't have to look that far for great writing. We have a lot of it here in the good old U.S.A."

"Such as, Mr. Cook?"

"Such as—" Brian Dexter Cook's blue eyes searched the ceiling of the Algonquin dining room, as he quoted from memory: " 'The cold passed reluctantly from the earth, and the retiring fogs revealed an army stretched out in the hills, resting. As the landscape changed from brown to green, the army awakened, and . . .' "

"Stop," Stephen Crane begged in mock horror. "You're embarrassing me, Brian Dexter Cook."

Brian shook his head firmly.

"A man who can write like that doesn't have to be embarrassed at all. Not ever. By anyone or anything."

Stephen Crane said no more but thanked him with his eyes.

They went on dining, enjoying each other's company. The minutes sped by. The day wore on. For Brian Dexter Cook it was a welcome rescue from the terrible state of mind he had been in.

A plague take all women. From the past to the present.

Particularly Miss Lois Weatherall.

Just exactly like Miss Linda Balfour with her coy feminine wiles and games.

Women weren't worth a feather or a fig.

Not with a war going on.

Now Brian Dexter Cook could not wait to get to Cuba.

The sooner, the better.

And the devil take the hindmost!

\*       \*       \*

Lois Weatherall reported to the office of William Randolph Hearst the afternoon of that same day. Her mood was even darker than Brian Dexter Cook's. But she held her chin high despite that, and she was determined to tell Mr. Hearst everything that had happened, save the very special part about falling in love with her target. Clearly, that would not do. Best to keep such things to one's self. It was a private matter entirely and had nothing to do with the policies or the well being of the *New York Journal*, did it?

Mr. Hearst heard her out as she sat in the same chair of that first meeting. The publisher stood at the windows overlooking the avenue, his hands clasped behind his back. A light rain had fallen once more; the sun was gone and the day was as suitably damp and miserable as Lois Weatherall's mood. Her heart was in her shoes. She could not quite eradicate the harsh words of Brian Dexter Cook nor the glare of utter contempt in his eyes in Mrs. Lanigan's parlor. That glare, that *look*, might very well stay with her forever.

When she had concluded her report, she fell silent.

There was no more to say. It was all up to Mr. Hearst now. She could only stare down at the floor, crestfallen. Also, she was tired. Very, very tired. And strangely deflated.

Mr. Hearst, without turning, grunted: "Stubborn,

eh? Unyielding, firm—no man's slave but his own, I suppose.''

Lois looked up, eyes widened. "Yes. I should say that about describes him, Mr. Hearst. You'd be wasting your time, I think, to pursue the matter any further.''

"Oh, you do, do you?'' William Randolph Hearst, rasped, turning. A very strange smile brightened his dour face. "Well, I'd say you were right, Miss Weatherall. To Hades with Brian Dexter Cook. Let him go his own way. I don't want him anymore.''

"I'm glad then. I'm sorry I couldn't do what you asked me to, Mr. Hearst. I'm afraid it wasn't my sort of thing—''

"Poppycock, Weatherall. You performed admirably. That stunt on the ferry was worthy of a Dick Davis. Fast thinking, resourceful, courageous. I admire you, young lady. So much so that I am about to take one more gamble with you. But a smart one, I think. After all, women read the *Journal*, too, don't they? I think they'd be rather interested in your view of the business in Cuba— you admire Nellie Bly. Then, by Jupiter, you will emulate Nellie Bly for me!''

Hearst thundered that last, bringing a clenched fist down atop his ornate table. An inkwell rattled; a pencil rolled.

Lois Weatherall stared at him wonderingly.

"You mean—you're saying—'' She collected

her wits and her words. "I don't understand what you mean—"

William Randolph Hearst stopped smiling. His dour features settled in a grim, unamused mold. His owl eyes slitted.

"I mean I am sending you to Cuba, all expenses paid, to cover the war for this paper. From a female's point of view. Do I make myself clear, Miss Weatherall? You are no longer on the Society Page."

Lois Weatherall shook; a joyous trembling began in her ankles, worked up to her knees, flooded her stomach, and traveled up to her heart and then her brain. No woman had ever had an opportunity like this—not ever—why, it was unheard of— unthinkable—a female where the fighting was— where she might get seriously hurt, even killed— why, it would be the first time ever in newspaper history that such a thing happened—what would people say?

She could not speak for long seconds.

"Well, Weatherall? I'm waiting for your answer. The chance of a lifetime. I'm sure you know that. A big gamble for me, but worth it if you've got the stuff. Got what it takes."

She swallowed and cleared her throat. Her chin tilted, as it always did when she was challenged. Her violet-shaded eyes sparkled.

"I'll do it, Mr. Hearst. I'll go. I've got what it takes."

"Splendid. I expected nothing less from you. I'll clear the decks for you with T. Rogers again and I'll arrange your travel date and all the details . . ."

She hardly heard him now. She wasn't listening anymore.

In her mind, only one simple truth stood out above all the other truths. One diamond-hard fact. One ironical masterstroke.

Mr. Brian Dexter Cook was not going to get rid of her so easily. And they had a score to settle. Cuba wasn't all that big—they were bound to meet again—to, to—she tried not to think about that.

But she was convinced once again of the venerable wisdom to be found in the Bible: "The Lord doth move in mysterious ways, his wonders to perform."

William Randolph Hearst had come up with a miracle.

She was going to Cuba, too!

Just as the United States Army and Navy and hordes of newspaperpeople and the rest of the world were at that moment, whether actually or vicariously, in thought and in print.

Just like Brian Dexter Cook was going.

Marvelous, foolish man.

She'd show him, God willing.

Show him that she wasn't to be taken that lightly.

The rain was still falling on the Hearst windows, but Lois Weatherall didn't care anymore about

that, either. The world had transformed into a very
sunny place, indeed. There were roses in the air.

And the sweet, fragrant smell of victory.

She had won.


   Miss Linda Balfour's carefully worded letter of
apology, which also invited Mr. Brian Dexter Cook
to tea that day, went unanswered. It arrived by
messenger at the Hotel Algonquin about fifteen
minutes after Brian had quit the premises in the
company of Stephen Crane. Both young men had
decided to spend the balance of the day on a
walking tour of the Times Square area. There was
so much to see and a great deal to share. Crane
was particularly interested in the book shops on
Eighth Avenue and along Broadway. Cook, familiar
with the neighborhood, was delighted to be his
guide. The rain bothered them not at all, for it was
light and pleasant. And he was thinking of a fine
little Italian restaurant near Columbus Circle which
might make Stephen Crane forget about his stomach just this once.

   Brian Dexter Cook did not return to the hotel
until well after eight o'clock. By that time it was
too late to respond to Miss Balfour's summons,
nor did he feel like calling her on the telephone.
His feelings about women had not changed one
iota. He was in that state of mind and heart where
he was convinced he was better off without them.
At least for the time being and at this stage of his

life. His day with Stephen Crane had been delightful and rewarding. Crane was a man who knew
much and had been many places—Brian had listened raptly. And the hours had sped by. Spaghetti
was out of the question, it developed, so they'd
had a steak dinner in Hennessy's Bar and Grille on
Seventh Avenue—which proved delightful, too. In
the end, they'd parted great friends and promised
to keep in touch with one another in the future.
Richard Harding Davis had been correct, as always.
Stephen Crane was a fine, sensitive man.

The *Marlboro* was due for an early morning
sailing, so Brian Dexter Cook completed his final
packing, readied what he would wear the first day
on board, and retired early. He was eager to be
gone.

His head was full of dreams, hopes, and ex-
pectations.

He deliberately kept his mind free of Miss Lois
Weatherall—as frightfully hard as that was to do.
One doesn't forget a vision quite that easily. And
whatever she was, Lois Weatherall was *that*. He
had never seen any woman quite so beautiful. He
had the acute feeling that he never would, either.
Sighing, he pounded his pillow and turned on his
side in bed. Almost unbidden, a poem from Robert
Louis Stevenson's *A Child's Garden of Verses*
came to his rescue and freed him of thoughts and
images of Lois Weatherall. Those lovely lines from

"The Land of Counterpane" that spoke to all children everywhere:

*When I was sick and lay abed,*
*I had two pillows at my head*
*And all my toys beside me lay*
*To keep me happy all the day . . .*

The lines were soothing, seemed apt and proper.

He was a newspaper reporter, but he was a soldier now, too.

Going into battle. Going to the Spanish-American War for the *New York Herald*. And Mr. James Gordon Bennett. Junior, of course. The first James Gordon Bennett, the Old Man, had died a long time ago.

The poem worked its magic. Lois Weatherall's fading face evaporated, dissolved, disappeared. He smiled happily. Contentedly.

Soon he was asleep. Peacefully asleep. No longer troubled. Or heartsore. The very young can never stay with misery too long. It is not their way. It is the strength of the young, if the weakness of the very old, who have nothing to fight back with.

Brian Dexter Cook wanted to get going, wanted to reach Cuba and begin his assignment. To forget the past and concentrate on the present. The future would take care of itself, as it always did.

Cuba was all that mattered now.

Cuba and the Spanish-American War.

*I was the giant great and still*
*That sits upon the pillow-hill*

*And sees before him, dale and plain,*
*The pleasant land of counterpane . . .*

Brian Dexter Cook slept like a baby on the eve of the greatest adventure of his life.

His history was still in the making.

# BOOK TWO

## RIDE TO THE SOUND
## OF THE BUGLES

". . . I did not want this war. I think everyone knows that. But now that we are committed, now that we are engaged with the enemy both on land and at sea, then let's put a stop to the whole terrible business. . . . I am certain the Almighty is with us . . . if I didn't believe that, I'm positive Teddy Roosevelt would! I never knew a man to think that God was on his side the way T.R. does . . ."

—*President William McKinley,*
*May 11th, to his wife, Ida Saxton*
*McKinley.*

# CUBA AND CORRESPONDENTS

The month of May yielded to June, and the three weeks which had literally shot by were so crammed with troop movements, wartime developments, and impending passages-of-arms that the whole world held its breath. No global event so occupied the minds and hearts of people as did the Spanish-American War that April and May of eighteen ninety-eight. Dewey and the Asiatic Fleet still bottled up Havana Harbor, holding Spain at bay in a guns-trained blockade that permitted nothing and no one to enter or leave the port. Rear Admiral Sampson still had not caught up with the elusive Admiral Pascual Cervera y Topete. The Spanish fleet had successfully eluded the North Atlantic Squadron and slipped into the landlocked harbor of Santiago de Cuba. This was in the closing days of the month and on May twenty-eighth Sampson's ships placed a strong blockading armada to the Spanish front outside the harbor, sealing off escape. It was a formidable checkmate of Cervera's forces. And now, as Sampson signaled the United States Army of his opponent's position, great plans were hastily made. The Army would prepare an expeditionary force to assault Santiago by land.

Major General William R. Shafter was assigned to handle this very important military maneuver. Toward that end, he framed logistics that would include fifteen thousand troops and all the artillery field pieces he could muster. In his multiple preparations, he included for use the First Cavalry Volunteer Regiment, the *ad hoc* striking unit which had been put into operation under the auspices and tutelage of Colonel Leonard Wood and none other than Teddy Roosevelt, now Lieutenant Colonel Theodore Roosevelt. Santiago de Cuba would be no strawberry festival. Spain had ringed it heavily from the surrounding low-lying hills with nine fighting forts garrisoned with their best soldiers. There was a railroad about a mile from the bay and beyond that nothing but wagon roads for travel.

General Shafter was no fool. He would send his expeditionary force into the coastal towns of Daiquirí and Siboney, near Santiago and away from the many guns of the many forts. Shafter was not going to waste American lives in a futile frontal attack. He was going to outflank Santiago de Cuba and then link up with the Cuban army that lay in the hills behind Santiago, led by General Calixto Garcia y Iniguez—General Garcia to all; the honest fighting man who was waiting for some word, any word, from his U.S. allies. Garcia had led the Cuban Army in revolt against the tyranny of Spain since the dark days of ninety-five, which had led up to this new war for his country. A man who had been a lawyer in civilian life, Garcia knew how to wait. Now Garcia waited, his troops spoiling for action against the oppressors. The message *must* come!

Santiago de Cuba lay at the very foot of the Sierra Maestra range on the southeastern coast of the country. It was four hundred and sixty miles southeast of Havana and that all-important blockade. Santiago was a shipping center for sugar, coffee, tobacco, and manganese, and the mining industry was taking a foothold now. The Morro Castle, a famous landmark, built to defend the harbor against British and French pirates in the days of the buccaneers, still thrust its stone battlements up from the sea. And now Santiago had become the battle zone of extremely crucial significance. General Shafter was certain that success in Cuba lay there. Lieutenant Colonel Roosevelt was of the same mind. "Bully, General! The Rough Riders can eat up ground like those low hills—wait and see if they can't!"

And keeping the peoples of the world abreast of all these developments, Americans particularly, were the daily dispatches rushed by land and sea to the big newspapers waiting back in New York—those papers with syndicates who could plant the same news and information in literally hundreds of dailies all over the country. So it was that Mr. Richard Harding Davis of the *Journal*, Mr. Brian Dexter Cook of the *Herald*, and Mr. Stephen Crane of the *World* sent their daily copy out, content with the knowledge that millions would read their stories the next day. As they did, so did a woman named Lois Weatherall, also associated with Hearst Papers; though not committed to a day-by-day coverage of the news from the battle zone, she submitted a weekly human-interest piece under the shocking title "As a Woman Sees the War," and her name was fast becoming a very familiar byline to readers of the *New York Journal*. American women cheered; Hearst sold a lot of newspapers. More than usual. Miss Weatherall had a knack for writing moving copy.

And the First Volunteer Cavalry, dubbed the Rough Riders, and their colorful commanders, Wood and Roosevelt, began to take on the dimensions and hues of heroes. America could not read enough about them. Dick Davis, Stephen Crane, Brian Dexter Cook, and Lois Weatherall did not skimp on their reportage of the activities of this carefree, galloping, hard-riding collection of ex-cowboys, soldiers of fortune, freedom lovers, Eastern playboys-turned-patriots, friends of T.R., and overgrown-boys-who-just-loved-a-good-fight.

If ever an outfit was spoiling for action in a war, the First Volunteer Cavalry was that outfit. They cleaned their weapons daily. The Rough Riders were itching to ride. To fight, to shoot.

They had the spirit; they had the horses. They had the expertise for war. All they needed was the opportunity. A golden chance.

It was inevitable that it should come.

Sooner or later.

There was a war going on, wasn't there? Right here in Cuba.

"Bound to be some ruckus before long," as Tex Whitover, the most raw-boned and rangy of all T.R.'s friends was wont to say almost routinely around the regiment to anyone who would listen.

Tex Whitover had been in Deadwood in the Dakota Territory the day Wild Bill Hickock was shot in the Number Ten Saloon by Jack McCall— way back in seventy-six, when Whitover was a mere stripling. He was no stranger to shoot-outs and action, either. He was on temporary leave from the Texas Rangers to serve with his old friend Colonel Teddy. Tex Whitover, age forty-five, might have been a model for the man who served as a Rough Rider in the FVCR: A hard rider and a hard shot.

There were many more very much like him.

Bachelors, loners, childless men, people of the plains and hills and ranch lands. Even the Eastern playboys, more anxious to do some good in the world than to fit a social pattern.

Only Lieutenant Colonel Theodore Roosevelt, their colorful field leader, was the exception to the typical Rough Rider. After all, Colonel Teddy was married and had five little tykes—but, then again, that figured, too. T.R. was always in a class by himself.

A real, genuine one-of-a-kind. A true-blue American.

Instead of sitting home by the fireside with his pipe and slippers or dawdling around the White House signing papers, here he was, out in the field, carrying an old horse pistol and raring to go. A man's man, T.R. Nothing mollycoddle about him.

Tex Whitover and all the rest of the men who were his comrades-in-arms, adored him. Revered him. He might have been their God.

So General William R. Shafter readied his expeditionary forces for the landings at Daiquirí and Siboney.

And the Rough Riders were ready for action, were champing at the bit.

For Brian Dexter Cook, the entire three weeks since his sailing on the *Marlboro* had been a great adventure. The greatest, really.

He had learned what it was to be a war correspondent.

And in the process he found what he was really looking for in this life, this world, this universe.

He wanted to be a man *first*.

Everything else came second.

Including his feelings for Miss Lois Weatherall . . .

Whom he had been dismayed to find scarcely a day behind him on his trip to Florida. Whom he now caught fleeting glimpses of wherever he turned or went on the streets of Jacksonville, where all the representatives of the press had gathered because the first American troops were debarking there by the trainload before moving down to Miami to prepare for the Cuban invasion. And the word had spread like wildfire among the male fraternity. William Randolph Hearst had executed another of his Famous Firsts—he had sent a reporter down to cover the war from a woman's viewpoint; a revolutionary notion which didn't seem to bother Richard Harding Davis at all. In fact, Dick Davis, once he espied Lois Weatherall filing her day's copy at the local telegraph office, had announced to one and all of his reportorial brethren: "By the Eternal—there goes the most beautiful creature I have ever seen! What say ye, Brian? Is that a pippin or is that a pippin?''

"She'll do," Brian agreed rather sullenly. He had told no one of his disastrous affair of the heart. Not even Dick Davis and Stephen Crane had as yet arrived at that stage of the game. "But she's *Journal*, so I suppose you'll have squatter's rights. Good luck to you, Dick. She seems your sort of woman—''

"Hold on now," Davis laughed. "Dear William Randolph has already informed me by discreet communication that I am to leave the lady to herself and not charm her into submission. She's here to write the story—''

"Do you always do what Hearst tells you to do?" Brian jibed.

"Not always. But this time I think I will. Miss Weatherall is far too beautiful. She would distract me no end.''

"You're the man to know that," Brian Dexter Cook agreed and turned away. He did not want to look at Lois Weatherall. All the other correspondents within earshot laughed heartily at that. Lois Weatherall was thus launched, unofficially, into a world which had only been inhabited by men—the newspaper world, with all its strict rules, mores, and taboos. It was well that she did not know most of them—she might have been doubly frightened and apprehensive.

Brian felt a pang seeing her like that. All at

once. The tall, lithe figure, the incredible profile, the Gibson Girl vitality and brightness. Memories assailed him, but he shook them off angrily.

It was just like Hearst to send a woman to Cuba. Exactly like him.

The man would do anything at all to sell his newspapers!

And now he had given Brian Dexter Cook a major problem all around. How was he to avoid Lois Weatherall? And get on with the war?

They were bound to cross paths one day soon.

As they did—in a manner totally unexpected.

Three days later, with the sun veritably melting the Jacksonville streets and bulletins coming steadily from New York and Washington as to the status of the Asiatic Fleet and North Atlantic Squadron, Brian Dexter Cook had his first opportunity to interview Lieutenant Colonel Theodore Roosevelt in the pyramidal tent in the huge bivouac area on the outskirts of town. The First Volunteer Cavalry Regiment was "roughing it" in a tent city of their own making, while the regular Army and a detachment of U.S. Marines were being comfortably housed in the city proper. The notion seemed to be to Teddy Roosevelt's liking. Never had Brian seen so many horses and so many men who looked as if they belonged both *with* horses and *on* horses. Before he reached the Colonel's tent, led by a uniformed orderly, he spotted more than one bowlegged trooper polishing saddle leather, cleaning sidearms and rifles, and generally honing up for battle. There was a pitch of preparedness in the air that Brian found quite exhilarating. This was an outfit that was obviously very ready to do something about the war. Whatever that might be. The air rang with lusty shouts, ribald male talk, campfire good humor, and camaraderie. Brian made a mental note to write about that very aspect in his next dispatch to the *Herald*. The public would relish it.

"Brian, my boy! It's good to see you. Bully, indeed!"

"Colonel—did you think only three weeks ago on Capitol Hill, in our talk at the cloak room, that we'd meet so soon again and the country would be at war?"

"I had a feeling—this old nose of mine never fails—McKinley had to move sooner or later. We all just helped him make up his mind by shoving him just a little. Sit down, my boy. Coffee to your liking?"

"Thank you, yes. I hope you're in the mood to talk about this thing. The *Herald* is waiting on your every word—even if this won't be exactly an exclusive for me—"

"Equal time for all, Brian. That's the American way."

"I couldn't agree with you more, Colonel. It

was something I never could make Mr. Hearst understand.''

They both sat down, Brian Dexter Cook on a camp chair across from the small card table propped between himself and the man he had come to see. Theodore Roosevelt, rimless glasses in place as ever, toothy smile still flashing, never looked more robust or adventurous to Brian Dexter Cook. This man who had begun life as a frail, sickly youth and then conditioned himself working on the ranch, hunting buffalo, and living the outdoor life was now in Army khaki from head to foot. His breeches were tucked into leather boots, and a heavy cartridge belt girded his waist with a holstered pistol in plain view. The kerchief at his tanned throat was more bandana than kerchief, worn with a cavalier air. The tent all about was festooned with maps and diagrams pinned to the sides. There was a small open fire on which stood a pot heating steadily over low-burning logs. Roosevelt was alone, and Brian appreciated that, too. It showed how much T.R. trusted him.

Roosevelt sat back in his chair and placed a hand on one knee. His genial face, crinkled as always, was carefully appraising his visitor. ''Hearst, eh? One of our great unhanged rascals. I must say you're looking damn fit, Brian. You ought to ride with us.''

''I will if you ever need me to. When the time comes.''

"I'm sure of that, my boy. Well, fire away. You had questions, you say? Americans want to know more about the Rough Riders?"

"All they can read about, sir." Brian could not help smiling back at this ingratiating man of infectious spirit. "Walking here through the camp, I must say I was impressed. There's a great esprit de corps. It's apparent to everyone, I think. You've got them on a fine edge, I'd say."

Roosevelt chuckled. A deep, warm laugh.

"Oh, they're more than ready. They want to bite off Cuba and spit it right into Manila Bay. And they will, I'm sure, when the time comes, as you say. Once the fleets give us the word that Havana is secure to the north and south, Shafter will send us in to take the ground and occupy. Mark these words, my boy. This will not be a very long war. Our forces are far too superior. Once we take Cuba by land—the thing will be done. I think Spain knows that, too. She's desperate. With General Garcia up in the hills behind Havana with his army—" The rimless glasses twinkled. "George Dewey made the difference, son, with that marvelous sweep the very first week of this affair. We've had them checkmated ever since. Do you play chess, Brian?"

"Yes, Colonel—may I quote you, sir, on all you have just said?"

"By all means. Quote until the rafters ring. I never make any bones about what I have to say.

You know me by now." Roosevelt chuckled once more. "In certain quarters of the country, do you know what they say *T.R.* stands for?"

Brian shook his head, smiling.

"Top Rebel, my boy. *Top Rebel*. And rather than consider that a disparaging remark, I'm proud of the designation. Damn proud. This country of ours got to where it is today because of rebels. Men like Washington, Jefferson, Lincoln, Andy Jackson, Ben Franklin. I am honored to be considered one of them."

"I should say so, Colonel—"

"But come, you really are interviewing the wrong man. Why, my command are the boys to talk to. There's a fine bunch for you. Real, live American galoots and buckaroos. The cream of the crop, Brian. Men you'd be honored to share a campfire with. And when trouble comes calling, you'll be glad to have them at your side. Men like Tex Whitover, Hank Slocum, Bart Cody, Old Doc Hawkins, Chesterton and Peabody and Indian Joe Jones—"

"How many Tex's and Hank's would you say there are, Colonel?"

"At least a dozen of each, possibly more, Brian."

Both men laughed and the tent seemed to rock. But it was only the abrupt entrance of a tall soldier who loomed before them. He had come with all the stealth of an Indian. Brian and Colonel Roosevelt stopped laughing. The tall man was a sergeant, as his stripes clearly proclaimed, and never had Brian seen a more erect individual. The man was ramrod straight, his Stetson brim turned upward in the old cavalryman style. The face beneath that brim was stone-hard, unsmiling, and the frostiest of blue eyes seemed to peer down at Brian— distastefully. A wide mouth was tugged in a crooked sneer. The nose was like a blunt instrument that could be used to hit somebody. Brian restrained an involuntary shudder. The sergeant was no valentine of any kind.

"Yes, Harkness, what is it?" Colonel Roosevelt barked.

"Begging the Colonel's pardon, sir." A rigid salute knifed the air.

The voice might have been a file scraped across a hard rock.

"Well?"

"Do you think it wise, Colonel, sir, to have non-military personnel in this tent with all the classified, secret information and data in plain view before him?" The man stood at attention all through this amazing query. Brian almost made a sound of anger, but Theodore Roosevelt merely shook him off and returned his attention to the sergeant.

"Sergeant Harkness." There was iron in T.R.'s voice now.

"Sir?"

"Your intentions are commendable, and your zeal to protect the best interests of the United

States—and myself—are beyond reproach. But, by God, Sergeant, trust me to be the better judge of whom I allow in my tent to see these things.''

"The Colonel is the best judge, I agree.''

"Thank you, Sergeant Harkness. Anything else on your mind?''

"Permission to withdraw, sir.''

"Permission granted.''

When Sergeant Harkness had saluted briskly, about-faced like well-oiled machinery and vanished from the tent, Brian Dexter Cook let out a low whistle. "I feel as if someone just walked across my grave.''

"Too soon for that, my boy.'' Roosevelt shrugged. "You don't approve of my fighting sergeant, Harkness?''

"I don't think I'd like to serve under him in any capacity. He seems inflexible and hard—like nails, I'd say. He must really drive both himself and his men.''

Roosevelt beamed in approval.

"You're a good judge of character, Brian. Sergeant Harkness wears the Congressional Medal of Honor when in dress uniform. He won it in the Indian Wars—the Sioux uprising. He saved a platoon of regulars single-handed, with nothing more than a Sharps rifle and fifty rounds of ammunition. I read the citation—he was highly recommended to me by the War Department. I didn't see any reason to refuse him when he volunteered for the regiment.''

"Do you now?''

"I have given him time to show me that his disciplinary measures and tactics are worth their salt. Till then, I admit I give him some leeway. I would have had the hide of any ordinary soldier who just suggested to me what he did.''

"So I would think.'' Brian Dexter Cook closed his notebook and set down his coffee cup. "Well, thanks, Colonel. I'll take no more of your time.'' He rose from his chair and put his notebook away.

"Any time, Brian. You are always welcome. I've my eye on you, too, my boy. You'll go far in this world if you keep minding the precepts of fair play and sportsmanship—and humanitarianism— which, I'm pleased to say, I have found in you in abundance since the day we first set eyes on each other. You're my kind of man, Brian Dexter Cook.''

As flushed as any schoolboy from such a grand compliment, Brian backed out of the tent. Colonel Roosevelt had returned to an examination of the rolled-out documents on the little card table. Brian was happy in another respect, too—he had more than enough to write about for Mr. Bennett and the *Herald* circulation—

"Hey, you—*Pretty Boy!*''

The sneering words, blurted out directly behind his back, made Brian Dexter Cook turn. Not easily. He whirled, knowing all too well who had uttered the remark. There was no mistaking that rasping, file-edged voice. Sergeant Harkness was smiling at him with insolent disobedience, taking his measure from head to foot. Since they were of equal height, the eye-to-eye aspects of the survey were downright ugly. Brian Dexter Cook controlled the angry flush trying to crawl up into his face where it could be seen. Still, he had to give the man an out—if he wanted one—although Brian was certain he didn't.

"I beg your pardon. Where you addressing me?"

The nearest human being to them was a tired cavalryman shining a belt buckle a good thirty feet away in front of his own tent. The sergeant made a great show of looking about, and then the frosty blue eyes resettled on Brian. A bugle sounded somewhere in the camp.

"Well, now, I'd say you were the only pretty face for miles around, Mr. Reporter. Wouldn't you?"

"Sergeant Harkness, let me inform you before—"

"Dutch Henry to you, Cook. They told me you were interviewing the Colonel today, and I don't like the idea. Not one little bit. I don't care for reporters in the very first place, and in the second, if this was my camp, I wouldn't let you people within five miles of the place. Do I make myself understood?"

Brian tried not to clench his hands into fists. It was not easy.

"Very well—Dutch Henry Harkness. What message is it that you are conveying to me?"

"Just this." Sergeant Harkness took a step forward. His wide, cruel mouth was within spitting distance of Brian's face. "If one scrap of secret information—one word about our operation here—leaks out or turns up in that sheet of yours— well, be warned, Pretty Boy. I'll come looking for you and I won't wait for the Colonel to tell me to keep my hands off you. Clear enough, Cook? I'm not taking any men into any traps set by the greasers because you and your kind have to write a lot of gossip."

"Dutch Henry," Brian said quietly. "I have no intention of betraying the Colonel's trust. Or anyone else's, for that matter. And now I have some advice for you—"

"And what might that be, Pretty Boy? You going to threaten me with your power of the press and all that guff?"

"My name is Brian Dexter Cook. Cook or Mr. Cook, to you, though I prefer the latter. I've heard about your medal from the Colonel. I think I'll look that up now, too. I'd like to know how you really won it. But hear me good, Dutch Henry. If you ever call me Pretty Boy again, within the hearing of others, I'll challenge you. Bare hands. And it's only fair to tell you I was on the boxing team at Cornell and never lost a fight. Clear enough, Dutch Henry?"

"Clear enough, Cook."

Sergeant Harkness' head tilted back and he laughed. An almost grudging laugh of admiration. The overhead sun glinted off a gold tooth in one corner of his mouth, the left canine. But when his head came down again, his lips were pressed together and the frosty eyes held nothing but hostility and menace in them.

"Go on," he rasped. "Get off the grounds. You've had your interview. Just watch yourself and remember what I told you."

Brain Dexter Cook flinched and was about to retort, but then he composed himself, remembered Teddy Roosevelt, and turning his back on Sergeant Dutch Henry Harkness, began to walk away.

But he was not to get off that lightly, it seemed.

Coming toward him, looking absolutely radiant and quite as if she had stepped down from the pages of *Harper's Bazaar*, Miss Lois Weatherall came striding. On her head was perched a colorful short-brimmed hat; her skirts rippled, and her full-bodied yet willowy figure was everything any normal man might desire. Any man, that is, save Sergeant Dutch Henry Harkness. Lois had not spotted Brian yet, for she was checking the fronts of all the tents lined up opposite one another, obviously looking for Colonel Roosevelt's billet. And Harkness, who had never heard of female reporters, made a huge mistake. He ripped out a low oath, one that Brian Dexter Cook could hear—and one that set his blood boiling. It would have angered any gentleman, but considering the special place in Brian's heart held by the beautiful apparition approaching, this one was unforgivable.

"What in hell—this the Barbary Coast or something? How did that trollop get past the sentries? I'll have their hides—"

Sergeant Dutch Henry Harkness had nothing for his pains but the surprise of his own lifetime. And then some.

The civilian he had disdainfully addressed as Pretty Boy, the reporter named Cook, suddenly resembled a whirlpool in motion.

He came around in a fluid, coordinated flurry of movement and, at the end of that movement, flew a roundhousing, arcing right hand doubled-up in the most compact of fists. The compactest.

This lightning bolt descended on Sergeant Harkness' unsuspecting jaw. When the fist met the jaw, there was a shuddersome sound of bone meeting bone. And Miss Lois Weatherall let out a shriek of dismay and shock. And in that precise instant, recognized Brian Dexter Cook. She had no way of knowing who the tall Army sergeant was who suddenly toppled backward, eyeballs rolling to show the whites of the eyes, and then fell flat like a chopped-down tree. And lay very still.

It was all over in an instant.

Dutch Henry Harkness did not know what hit

him until much later. He had never met a flying, fighting whirlpool before.

He had also underestimated Brian Dexter Cook.

A man who would do anything for a lady.

Dare anything.

Even if she chanced to be the lady who had broken his heart.

Unforgettably, and for the time being, irreparably.

# FLORIDA AND FRIENDLY ENEMIES

Later that same day, much later, Brian Dexter Cook was in a confused state of mind. He had filed his copy for the Roosevelt interview at the local telegraph office and then wandered about the Jacksonville streets till he found a small saloon off the main stem of the city. A place of low lighting, with wooden tables and cane chairs and potted plants, it was a Spanish-style bar, more of a *cantina* than anything. And the patrons seemed to be neighborhood gentry. He saw no one that he knew, not even a soldier. And he was glad. He wanted to be alone to sort out his thoughts. Even Richard Harding Davis would have taxed him this evening, no matter how gay and bright Dick's company always was. Brian Dexter Cook had a great deal to think about. There was a guitar playing softly somewhere in the darkened recesses of the bar, and he liked that, too. Dimly, he recognized the strains of a slow-tempo version of "The Battle Hymn of the Republic." He was not too surprised at that—patriotism was sweeping the country. Why not Florida, too, with the United States Army on its very doorstep?

He ordered a bottle of Napoleon brandy from a sleepy-eyed bartender, ignored the other patrons at the bar, and went back to his quiet table. The guitar throbbed mournfully, matching his mood.

Small wonder in that. It had been a bad scene on the camping grounds that afternoon, and he had played his role gracelessly. Never mind that he had defended Miss Lois Weatherall's good name and cold-cocked the meanest man he had known so far. Sergeant Dutch Henry Harkness had had it coming—but the reactions of dear Miss Weatherall had been completely unexpected and far from thankful. He realized she could not have known what triggered his assault on Harkness, but even so—his pleasure at seeing her so close again had rapidly been extinguished by her immediate behavior and her fiery speech of outrage.

"You brute! You struck that man when he wasn't looking! Oh, Brian, how could you? And I thought you were a gentleman—"

He could not answer her just then.

She had rushed up to him, defiantly, that perfect chin tilted, the violet-shaded eyes filled with contempt for him. And then she was by him, kneeling to the fallen Sergeant Harkness, trying to revive him with a series of murmured pleas, and cradling his head in her arms. The sergeant's Stetson hat had rolled and his close-cut military haircut showed a pelt of red hair. Brian Dexter Cook could bear to see and hear no more. He turned, speechlessly, and strode away without looking back. "Coward!" Lois Weatherall cried out. But he was not to be stopped. He swept by the tired soldier shining the belt buckle, the soldier did not try to intercept him—which was but another indication that Sergeant Dutch Henry Harkness was not the most popular non-commissioned officer in camp. In fact, the cavalryman winked at Brian as he passed.

And that was that.

He left the bivouac area unimpeded, not concerned at all about Harkness' good health. Within him, anger rolled; his mind was blazing. Damn the woman! Once again she had set him off on a bad tangent, demoralized his resolve—and blast William Randolph Hearst for sending a woman into a man's world when she ought to be at home taking care of a man and a family. Or owning up to the truth that war was no sane place for any female at all. Particularly Miss Lois Weatherall, the brazen-faced liar and hypocrite. *Coward*, was he? *Brute?*

It was in this frame of mind that Brian Dexter Cook consumed nearly three-quarters of a full bottle of Napoleon brandy. And lost all track of time, place, and his own position in the scheme of things. Just as he had that awful night he left Mrs. Lanigan's parlor to lose himself in a haze in some ratty saloon, he now found himself drifting off into intoxication. He no longer heard the guitar music, nor had he become aware of how the *cantina* had filled; masculine and feminine voices mingled and blurred in a medley of words. All kinds of words. And suddenly, there was a woman again. Squeezing herself into the corner next to him. He smelled sweetness, like the aroma of freshly cut flowers. He blinked, turning slowly. To come face-to-face with an extraordinary countenance. A face he thought he might have seen in one of those Spanish paintings by Velasquez or Goya or—was it simply great beauty striking the eye of the beholder?

"Do you wait for someone, *Americano muy hermoso?*"

"No," he said thickly, blinking again so that the stunning face so close to his would come into focus. "You call me handsome—I am studying Spanish—I know some words—*señorita*—"

"*Bueno*, then. We will talk. But not in Spanish. I speak English to you—yes? I much prefer it."

"No," he said again. "I'm not waiting for anyone. Welcome, dear *señorita*." He got hold of himself, his strong will fighting off the effects of far too much brandy. He narrowed his eyes, and the face of the woman, so close, cleared up almost magically.

A perfectly heart-shaped face. Wide, sensuous eyes, darker than midnight. A nose of slightly flared nostrils indicating great strength of character and passion. A mouth that was a scarlet invitation. Long, trailing blonde hair of a texture so fine, so like gossamer that it nearly seemed silver. The flesh was olive-skinned, but so smoothly textured as to seem a mask. From one delicate ear dangled a huge golden ring no thicker than a strand of hair. And bared shoulders ended just above surging mounds of rippling breasts tightly imprisoned in a black bodice spangled with beads. The woman glittered.

"You are most kind. You seemed so all alone— and you are so *magnifico*—it makes little sense that you are not with a woman."

"Drink?" He gestured to the bottle of brandy.

"No, *señor*—I never drink—I do not need such things. What are you called, *Hermoso?*"

He laughed. "Not that, dear *señorita*. But I do have three names. Brian Dexter Cook—choose anyone you wish."

Her low laugh was a light, silvery ripple that fell pleasantly on his ears. And the aroma of sweet,

fresh flowers stirred something within him. He
began to feel better. Much, much better. Miss Lois
Weatherall's irritating image shimmered and dissolved into nothing.

"I have five names, Brian Dexter Cook—"
Never had his own name sounded more like music.
"Rita Rozales Portago Maria de Sanchez. But I
am Rita Sanchez to all. I have never seen you in
here before."

"I have never been in here before—what is this
place—I don't remember—"

Her wide smile revealed teeth as white as ivory
piano keys.

"It is a *cantina*. *El Pato Blanco*—do you
comprehend?"

"*Sí, sí*, Rita. The White Duck." He set his
brandy glass down and put his hands to his temples.
Suddenly, a great weariness had come over him.
"I, dear lady, am very tired. Forgive me—"

"There is nothing to forgive, my Brian. You
have worked hard—long and hard—and you are
tired—there are rooms here, *querida*. Would you
like to sleep? It can be arranged—you see, *mio
tio*—my uncle, Manuel—owns this establishment.
It would be nothing to find you a room. . . ."

Brian Dexter Cook could not have said what he
replied to that. Nor could he have successfully
recalled all that happened after this beautiful Rita
Sanchez suggested a lodging for the night. Not if
his life had depended upon it. Or if he had to give

testimony in open court. Suffice to say, in a haze
of brandy, a blur of images, a transition of light to
dark, dark to light again, he was no longer sitting
in a darkened place, seeing shadowy figures and
hearing faint, far-off voices. Suffice to say, later,
he knew not how much later, he felt himself prone,
lying on his back. And someone was moving near
him, removing his shoes and stockings and then
his trousers. He never knew when his coat jacket
had been removed. And suddenly all was quiet,
and there was only a faint rustling sound and a
woman's murmuring voice in the great stillness
somewhere. He felt buoyant, airy, weightless. He
tried to peer upwards into a great void of darkness.
And then there was light—moonlight, really—
slanting across a floor, touching the bed on which
he lay. And the aroma of those flowers came to
him once more. He did not move. He did not stir.

The moonlight caught a movement of something.
A flitting shadow.

He stirred sleepily, eyes opening gradually.

He saw the pale blur of a shapely white figure,
the rolling, curving contours of a female form.
Silvery blonde hair shone in the ghostly rays of the
full moon hanging out there somewhere.

Then he felt her get into the bed, next to him.
And all at once he realized, without fear, that he
was totally naked, divested of every stitch of
outerwear. And the warm, pulsating flesh of a
woman was slowly grinding into his own body,

nestling next to him, snuggling. A cool arm encircled his waist. Gentle, skillful fingers traveled, splaying downward, touching him. Exciting him. There was hardly any protest or fight in him. His loins convulsed. The fine hand had closed over him, feeling him, stroking him, cupping him.

Her voice came to him out of the darkness. Out of his dreams. Out of his most exorbitant fancies. And good nights.

"Oh, Brian, *mi querida* . . . you will make love to Rita, yes? That would be so nice . . . and so very desirable . . ."

He could not speak. His senses were rioting, hammering.

She understood. She was all woman, all knowing and instinctive.

He twisted to meet her as her scalding thighs parted. The aroma of the flowers was overpowering, triumphing over the brandy and the fumes of his private debauch. His invasion of her was total.

With a fierce, exultant whisper of joy, Rita Sanchez sank her white teeth into his shoulder as her tongue flicked out like a darting snake. His hungry hands dug into the broad, bell-shaped arch of her full thighs. He surged, erupted, and exploded, driving her downward in a frenzied, thrusting lunge of all of his well coordinated muscles.

"*Dio . . . Dio . . .*" Rita Sanchez moaned. "Oh, my beautiful Brian . . . what are you doing to me? . . ."

Brian Dexter Cook hammered down at her, unmercifully. A wild, insane joy and confusion instilled within him the power of a god on Mount Olympus. Also, he could not see the lovely face of Rita Sanchez. Darkness was all around him; anger and hurt and hunger were the triple components of what emanated from his lips next.

"Oh, Lois, Lois . . . I love you, darling . . ."

Beneath him, Rita Sanchez smiled a smile he could not see, even as her ample body twitched and responded to his deep thrusts of flame and passion. It did not matter, not one bit.

These *Americanos* were all so much alike, even this big, beautiful Brian: men who could not release their true feelings until the wine and the brandy and the distance from the loved one made them behave like this—so hungry for a woman, so demanding.

It was just as well she had found out so soon.

It would make things that much easier to deceive this beautiful *Norteamericano*, without compunction, without regrets.

It must be done—for Spain, the lovely land of her birth.

*Sí*, this golden man must be tricked.

So that Cuba could be free again.

Of everything and everyone that came from *Los Estados Unidos*.

God's truth, Holy Mother!

\*     \*     \*

Brian Dexter Cook lay fast asleep on the rumpled bed. His face was turned to the soft, fluffy pillow, his mass of golden blonde hair falling down his forehead. Rita Sanchez lifted herself quietly from her position alongside him, now certain that nothing short of a fire alarm would awaken him. Her nubile, fully developed body crossed the room to where she had placed all his garments. They were hung over a wooden chair. The moonlight would be enough to see by. There was no need to turn up the lamp. The stealth of her movements, her intensity, was almost equal to the amount of passion she had bestowed upon Brian Dexter Cook. He had dropped off into slumber, thoroughly spent, drained of all his energy. He had not made such love to a woman, any woman, since an historic fraternity party during his Cornell University days—when a rather buxom housewife from Ithaca had lured him into the bushes on campus and literally seduced him to a fare-thee-well. He had responded, of course, more than creditably, but there had been no sexual encounters for Brian Dexter Cook since that night over three years ago. And now Rita Sanchez had plucked the benefits and harvest of his long abstinence from lovemaking. The *Americano* had serviced her most admirably—*Dio*, she yet ached pleasurably from his touch and his strength and his passion.

By moonlight, she carefully and deftly went through all his pockets, those in his coat jacket,

his trousers, his white shirt. She inspected his
billfold, examining its contents as if her life depended upon what she would find there. In truth, it
did.

She was not looking for money. Or diamonds or
jewelry. Or any such valuables.

Brian Dexter Cook slept on, peacefully, blissfully.

The moonlight was steady and unrelentingly glaring as Rita Sanchez continued her intense search
of his clothing.

The midnight-black eyes shone in the glare.

The bewitchingly voluptuous body trembled with
anticipation.

The slender, tapering fingers raced, probed,
explored.

There was so little time left—now.

She must hurry.

Before it was too late for Spain.

And Cuba.

Brian Dexter Cook, all unknowingly, had been
the center of conversation much earlier that day.
Had he not yielded to the luxury of the grape, his
ears might have rung. For many people found
much to discuss in relation to the representative of
the *Herald*. His encounter with Sergeant Dutch
Henry Harkness, however fleeting and brief, became a *cause célèbre*, mainly because Sergeant
Harkness, Lois Weatherall, Colonel Theodore
Roosevelt, and a tired cavalryman named Herbert

Riddle found much in the affair to interest them all. A great deal, in fact.

For one thing, Miss Weatherall was on the spot when Sergeant Harkness opened his eyes at last to find the sun shining down on him. He had what is known as a ceiling view of things. When he saw Lois Weatherall's incredibly lovely face, he was instantly beguiled. And masking his rage at being bested by a pretty-faced newspaperman, he played the injured party—masterfully. As Lois assisted him to his feet, he quickly framed a cover-up story to account for his fall from grace. He also realized that his initial judgment of the lady he had seen coming toward them was a monstrous error. He did know a lady when he saw one. Also, his jaw still ached where Brian had fetched him a superior blow. He would not soon forget the humiliation. Neither would Pretty Boy Cook, by God.

"Thank you kindly, ma'am. Did you see that fellow cold-deck me?"

"Yes, I did. And it was downright terrible—it's not like him, really. I thought he was such a fine gentleman—are you all right, Sergeant? Sergeant . . ."

"Harkness, ma'am. Henry Harkness. At your service and obligated to you for your kind consideration." Harkness scooped up his fallen Stetson and grimly reset it upon his head. His sharp eye had caught Herbert Riddle trying to ease back into his tent unobserved. "Just a minute, Private Riddle!

Stand fast." Riddle almost dropped the polished belt buckle in his surprise and haste. Lois Weatherall frowned. "Are you truly all right, Sergeant Harkness? I have an appointment to see Colonel Roosevelt, but I won't leave you if you need assistance."

"Now, never you mind, ma'am." Harkness grinned broadly and pointed a bony forefinger at the large pyramidal tent up the company street. "You go on about your business. Colonel Teddy's tent is right there. Takes more than a sneak punch to put down Mrs. Harkness' boy Dutch Henry. I'd be obliged to know your name. Someday I hope to return a favor for your kindness." The frosty blue eyes were sweeping over Lois Weatherall in a masculine survey that was not altogether attractive to the lady. But she smiled, hoping she had misunderstood. "I am Lois Weatherall and part of the newspaper corps down here, Sergeant Harkness."

"Well, now, that is most amazing. I do declare. Thanks again, Miss Weatherall. Till we meet again."

She could say no more to that and hastily beat a retreat, going toward the pyramidal tent. Harkness watched her go, noted the thoroughbred posture and carriage, and nodded to himself. Then he remembered Herbert Riddle and, turning smartly on one heel, marched up to the waiting private who now stood at quaking attention before his own tent.

"Riddle!" Harkness made the name sound like an accusation.

"Yes, Sergeant."

"Why aren't you at mess like everyone else in this man's army?"

"Wasn't hungry. I'm not feeling so good, Sergeant."

"Oh?" Harkness, inches taller, circled warily around his littler prey. "You see anything that didn't set too well with you, Riddle?"

"No, Sergeant."

"You're sure now?"

"Yes, Sergeant."

"Good. Keep it that way. If I was to hear anything about two people, a non-com and a civilian having some kind of disagreement, why, I would naturally think the story came from you, Riddle. Now, wouldn't I?"

"Yes, you would, Sergeant. But it wouldn't come from me. I keep to myself about anything like that. Honest, Sergeant. On my mother's grave—"

"That's just fine, Riddle. Keep it that way." Deliberately, Harkness turned his back on the little man. "Go on about your business. Go polish some more brass. *Dismissed!*"

He could hear Herbert Riddle scurrying gratefully into the tent to escape him. He smiled to himself, but his frosty blue eyes were leveled down the company street at the entrance of Colonel

Roosevelt's tent. This Weatherall filly was something, all right. A real peacherino. He'd have to look into that when he got the chance. But for now, there was Mr. Brian Dexter Cook to consider. He had a score to settle with Pretty Boy. Cold-decking him like that when he wasn't looking! Still, he had to admit, it was a powerful wallop. Sergeant Dutch Henry Harkness, who spoke a different brand of English when he conversed with officers, ran a dry tongue over his lower lip. He concealed the ache of his bruised jaw, turned smartly, and stalked down the street, away from the pyramidal tent.

He was a grand-looking military man. He had walked erect and proudly since the day he had joined the Army. Way back in '89. Now, at thirty years of age, he was every inch the soldier. Proud of his Congressional Medal of Honor and hungry for promotion, he kept his frosty eye ever fixed on officer's straps. The day would come for him—he was sure of that. This business in Cuba was the big chance. Hell, a professional soldier waited for wars to come. Peacetime armies never afforded any opportunities for advancement. But with T.R. and these Rough Riders . . . Harkness's eyes gleamed in the sunlight. He intended to kill at least fifty Cuban greasers when the regiment got to where the fighting was. But first—

There was Pretty Boy to take care of. Yes, indeedy.

College boys had always angered Sergeant Dutch Henry Harkness.

He had never gotten past the fifth grade in public school, having to pitch in and help work the old man's farm back in Kansas.

It was a sacrifice he had never forgiven his father and mother for. Not ever. Education, proper education, the lack of it, Harkness was convinced, had kept him back, kept him low on the social and economic scale of American life. The Army had been his only salvation. His real home.

The Army was going to get him everything he wanted out of life. Officer's straps, more money, lots of travel, and maybe some filly like this Miss Weatherall. Women like that needed a man like him—not some Pretty Boy with a soft voice and fancy manners. Damn mollycoddle!

Harkness was whistling as he marched down the street.

Any soldier—or civilian, for that matter—would have recognized the melody of "When Johnny Comes Marching Home Again" . . .

*Hurrah, hurrah.*

Sergeant Dutch Henry Harkness couldn't wait to get to Cuba.

Damn, but he was going to kill a lot of greasy-haired Cubans. Lousy pigs. He was as sure of that as he was that President McKinley was President of these United States. The good old U.S. of A.

Which so proudly he hailed . . . at the twilight's last gleaming.

The sergeant always walked tall, wherever he might be.

But he was truly one of the smallest men alive.

"I'm afraid you're in grave error, Miss Weatherall." Colonel Theodore Roosevelt took off his rimless glasses and began to wipe them with a soft white rag. "You've misinterpreted the—ah, brawl—which you have described to me. I'm afraid I witnessed the whole affair from this very tent. You see, my hearing is extremely sharp. Extremely. I once heard a coyote stalking me and my mount on a very windy day back in Dakota—"

Lois Weatherall made a moue. "I beg your pardon, Colonel. I did see Mr. Cook hit that sergeant—"

"Indeed, you did. A magnificent blow. Worthy of Gentleman Jim Corbett himself. But, pshaw—you did not hear the insult offered you by Harkness. Brian Dexter Cook did. And he responded as any true gentleman would. I would have kept all this to myself, but just now you seemed to suggest that you despaired of the young man's conduct. I can't have that. The truth must out, dear lady, as it always does, in the end."

"For heaven's sakes, Colonel Roosevelt. What could the sergeant have said? I never met the man before today—"

Roosevelt chuckled, then frowned. His crinkly face was now almost rueful. "No matter. Sergeant Harkness, who is a good soldier but has much to learn about people—women, particularly—described you aloud, in no uncertain terms. Cook took exception to that, as you so clearly saw. Bully for the boy! And well done altogether."

"But Colonel Roosevelt—"

"Now, now, my dear. The term the sergeant applied to you was not vulgar or profane—merely inaccurate. He called you a *trollop*. I'm sure you're familiar with the word, being a reporter and all."

Lois Weatherall's matchless complexion flamed. Not from the word, no, but from her gross stupidity, her complete injustice to Brian Dexter Cook. The poor man—once again she had betrayed him, marking him all those terrible names she had called him—*coward, brute*—and all he had done was defend her honor!

"Oh, Lord," she wailed, feeling acutely miserable. "Brian will never talk to me again. And who's to blame him?"

"I wouldn't dwell on that too much, Miss Weatherall. He's a very young man and you are so beautiful—" Colonel Theodore Roosevelt placed his polished glasses once more on his nose. "Now, I've done my Christian duty. You have your interview and I have defended a young man I like very much. Very much indeed. I'm sure you both can set this matter right between the two of you." He chuckled. "I would say an apology is in order, wouldn't you?"

Lois Weatherall could only nod, eyes misting.

"And you will do that for me, Miss Weatherall? Apologize?"

"Oh, yes, yes! And thank you so much, Colonel. You've helped me from making a bigger fool of myself than I have already!"

"On you, my dear, it looks very well indeed. And now—shoo. Scat. Leave me to these enormous plans and dreams for a conquest in Cuba. Go write your story or whatever. Just tell the American people the Rough Riders will not let them down. They can bank on us all. From the moment we set foot on Cuban soil."

"I will, Colonel Roosevelt. I promise you that."

Long after she had quit the pyramidal tent and walked back to her waiting transportation, a horse-drawn surrey with a black driver from the hotel staff, she could not get Brian Dexter Cook out of her mind. She passed many a soldier who respectfully waved to her in greeting and cast admiring glances as she walked on, but no one halted her or tried to be rude and offensive. There was a fine, tangy feel in the atmosphere, a sense of many men and much equipment being readied for some grand adventure, but she did not think much about that, either. Not just now. She would set that down later when she wrote her piece for Mr. Hearst, who had been ever so supportive and enthusiastic about her

maiden copy. No, Brian Dexter Cook was on her
mind.

As usual.

As he had been since the very first day that she
had set eyes upon him. Oh, what an exasperating
man!

And she had to fall in love with him!

More fool she.

When she stepped into her waiting surrey, the
black driver beaming approval at her and doffing
his stovepipe hat, anyone within sight of her would
have unanimously agreed that she was quite the
loveliest creature alive. One woman in a million.

Even Brian Dexter Cook would have had to
admit that.

Whatever his tangled-up feelings were.


Rita Sanchez stood at the foot of the bed in the
dark back room and stared down at the sleeping
man who had been her lover so long and ardently
this challenging night. The moonlight was gone
now.

The gray tinge of dawn came creeping, leaving
ghostly, eerie light across the wooden floor. Rita
Sanchez had covered her nakedness with a worn
and faded robe on which the flower patterns had
long since lost their bright colors. She looked
incomparably regal and majestic in spite of the
robe. The long silvery hair, the olive-textured face,
the striking features, the imposing contours of her

soft but firm body, all made her as much of a beauty in her class as Lois Weatherall was in yet another category. Latin America and America could have been well served by both these very young women. They were bona fide prototypes.

Rita Sanchez held up her right arm and stared at her hand.

Her fingers were closed about a simple kitchen knife, one whose curved blade was fully eight inches long. A meat-cutter.

She had found nothing of what she was seeking on this golden man who had come off the street into the *cantina*. This newspaper person who should have had some information about his person. Vital information, for Rita Sanchez and her accomplices knew that the Yankee Colonel with the peculiar name—Roosevelt—was giving important news and details to these men who printed things in papers. But Brian had had nothing in the pockets of his clothes, save for personal effects.

So there was nothing left but death for him. And disposal of his foolish body in some back alley far from this neighborhood. One more drunken news-paperman and the local *policia* would be satisfied.

Rita Sanchez walked toward the sleeping man, coming around the bedposts like a wraith. She moved like a great jungle cat.

The kitchen knife arced upward, slowly.

Ritz Sanchez was barely breathing.

The midnight-black eyes were expressionless.

She was Death, walking.

In the form of a beautiful woman.

Always one of the Grim Reaper's cleverest disguises.

For all men everywhere.

Brian Dexter Cook was no exception to the rule.

# TAMPA AND TOGETHERNESS

Fate, that indefinable phantom who so governs the lives of all mankind, the great and small, the famous and infamous, the rich and poor, now stepped into the life of Brian Dexter Cook. He lay sleeping as defenseless as any child, while the woman with the murderous knife stood over him at bedside. One second longer, one more tick of the clock, and Brian Dexter Cook would never have known what struck him down. Not in this world, at any rate.

There came a low, muffled knock at the door.

Rita Sanchez, in mid-movement, checked her hand and the descending knife. For a long moment, her heart stopped beating as her dark eyes flew to the door. The soft knock came again, more insistent this time, and a man's voice muttered hoarsely: "*Rita—vamonos—pronto! Soldatos aqui!*"

It was her Uncle Manuel's voice, and his message chilled her to the bone. Soldiers at the White Duck—at this hour of the day? *Dio*—what had gone wrong?

Quickly she hurried to the door. Brian had not stirred. She whipped the portal open. Uncle Manuel, his fat, wrinkled, moustached face showing two black, popping eyes, motioned her quickly into the hallway with its lone bulb hanging from a cord. He was perspiring freely.

"*Por que?*" Rita whispered anxiously.

Uncle Manuel wrung his hands. "They come— two soldiers—"

"Speak Spanish, Uncle. You make yourself much clearer," she snapped.

So he did. And in pure Castilian he explained that two soldiers were out in the bar, accompanied by a civilian, inquiring the whereabouts of Brian Dexter Cook, the man he was certain Rita had taken to her bed in her business of spying. The description of Brian had been far too accurate. Tall, blue-eyed, golden-blonde hair, very well-built, clean-cut. Ritz Sanchez calmed her uncle

down with a smile. "*De nada, tio,* we are safe. I
have done nothing. The man has enjoyed a night
with Rita. Do not be alarmed. He had too much to
drink. Tell them to wait; I shall be out in a moment.
He still sleeps—I won't wake him yet."

Her uncle heaved a monumental sigh of relief
and crossed himself.

"Come, then. Quickly. Relieve their minds.
Thank God you did not do anything yet we both
would have faced a firing squad for."

"Go. I will be only a moment." Uncle Manuel
fled down the hallway, his barrel-round body still
quaking, muttering under his breath.

Rita Sanchez did not know Richard Harding
Davis, but she recognized solemnity, suspicion,
and a threat when she saw them. The two burly
soldiers flanking him were carrying rifles. As they
stood waiting in the bar, they clearly indicated to
her just how little trust they placed in Spanish-
speaking people. It was a curse of the war now.
Everyone and everything Spanish, Mexican or
Cuban, was suspect.

Richard Harding Davis, the connoisseur of feminine beauty, however, smiled and bowed slightly
from the waist at sight of the sultry, dark-eyed
Rita Sanchez. Even wrapped in her faded robe,
she was awesome. Or perhaps because of that. The
two soldiers, mere privates but also men, kept
their faces respectful as they guardedly kept close

watch on the premises of the *cantina*. The interior of the grimy bar was ugly and dark.

"Forgive me, dear lady. Your uncle has informed us that our friend is with you. I am glad to hear that. I have been worried about his welfare all day. It is necessary, I am afraid, that you tell him we are here. He must come with us."

"*Americanos*—" Rita Sanchez decided to play her part to the hilt, the one they would expect of her—the loose lady of easy morals, and a Spaniard to boot. "Your gentleman and I—an affair of the heart—we have spent the night together in each other's arms. Is that not done when men and women like each other very much?"

Davis smiled, shaking his head, but he was still on the alert.

"I'm the last man to do this, God only knows, but I must break up your beautiful friendship. Mr. Cook is wanted elsewhere."

"At such an ungodly hour? The dawn of another day—"

"Mr. Cook is a newspaperman attached to the United States Army. That army is moving out right now. At the crack of dawn. For Tampa, the next marshaling point. Surely you know there is a war going on. Mr. Cook can't be left behind." Rita Sanchez concealed the quickening of her heart at this information so loosely rendered. Her dark eyes glinted.

"He is sleeping like a baby, but I shall awaken him."

"Thank you. That would be very good of you. Please excuse this show of arms." He gestured to the waiting soldiers. "But this part of town does not have the most savory reputation. Colonel Roosevelt deemed it advisable that I bring these men along, once I realized that Brian was missing and hadn't been seen since early yesterday."

"He must mean a great deal to you—Brian."

"He does. And the sooner I clap eyes on him, the better. Please fetch him. Would you rather I came with you?"

"No, no," she said quickly. "I will do that. After all—" And here she smiled a smile that would set a man's boots on fire. "I would wish to say good-bye to him—alone."

"As you wish, *señorita*."

When she had gone once more, Richard Harding Davis had to mentally congratulate Teddy Roosevelt and his knowledge of people. Knowing of Brian's falling out with the most beautiful woman he had ever seen and gauging that he would go out on the town and probably get roaring drunk, and with the plans for the troops to move out early in the morning—well, when Dick Davis reported the young man's absence from his hotel and the telegraph office and all the other familiar daily habitats for the gentlemen of the fourth estate—old T.R. had called the shot. So he had reacted to the emergency, assigned two armed privates to Dick Davis, and given him carte blanche on a sweep of the town's drinking places. *El Pato Blanco* had not been too hard to find. Closed or not, Dick Davis had roused Uncle Manuel, for gossip about a golden-haired white man on a drinking spree had been picked up along the route of search. Dick Davis had been truly worried. Brian, for all his brains and cleverness, was very new to this sort of thing, he knew.

One of the soldiers glanced at him when Rita departed in a gliding walk. "I wouldn't trust a woman that looks like that one does, Mr. Davis. She's no angel for my money."

"No, Cassidy, neither would I," Richard Harding Davis agreed, reaching for a cigarillo from his inner coat pocket. "But you're wrong, you know. She is an angel. But certainly a fallen one."

The other soldier, Simpson by name, guffawed appreciatively.

They all waited for Rita Sanchez to come back with the man they had been looking for half the night with a growing fear.

A round-faced clock behind the bar showed the hour of seven.

It was getting late. A new day was dawning for everyone.

The troop trains, loaded for Tampa, would be

leaving at eight o'clock sharp. Time was running out.

The Spanish-American War could not wait, either.

"Dick, I don't know what to say—"

"Don't say anything. You would have done as much for me, I'm sure. Besides, things have been fairly dull around here."

"I feel like the perfect fool—"

"You are, Brian, my boy. But I dare say you had an evening to remember. That was a great deal of woman back there."

"Rita—I hardly knew who she was until she awakened me with word you were outside waiting for me with the troopers. Lord, the brandy I drank last night would have floated a battleship."

"Indubitably. Tell me. Do you have any memory at all of this woman? Surely you must have talked to her at some time or other before the fun began—"

"Please don't josh me about this, Dick. I feel I must have behaved like an animal. My body is sore all over."

"Then I won't ask. As long as you didn't give away any valuable military secrets."

"I beg your pardon?"

"Spies, Brian, my boy; spies. There was talk that Florida and the environs would be filled with such people. There is a war on, as you know. There are many, many Spanish-born citizens in these parts who just might feel it their duty to fight for their homeland in that peculiar fashion known as spying.''

''Rita wouldn't—she couldn't—not a woman like her—''

''Really? What do you know about women like her, you wooly lamb? You're a babe in the woods at this sort of thing.''

Brian Dexter Cook leaned his head back against the leather-bound cushions of the carriage and closed his eyes. His whole body was strangely relaxed and warm. Despite a throbbing head that told of too much alcohol in his system, he had not entirely forgotten all that had passed between himself and Rita Sanchez. The threshing thighs, the scalding stomach and breasts—a tight smile crossed his mouth. Cassidy and Simpson, the two armed privates up front, guiding the horse-drawn carriage back to camp, were both harmonizing in a low duet. Stephen Foster's ''My Old Kentucky Home'' had never sounded better.

''Not anymore, old man. Not anymore. The lady was much woman, as the Spanish say. It was an education of sorts.''

''Bravo, Brian. Bravo. That's the way to handle these matters. Better reality with a Rita than moonshining over Miss Weatherall.''

''I'll thank you not to mention her name, Dick.''

''Sorry.'' Dick Davis shrugged. ''Well, are you now ready for the great pull-out? There's lots of activity been going on while you were pleasuring yourself at *El Pato Blanco*.''

''You said as much. Where is the army headed?''

''Tampa, Mr. Cook,'' Richard Harding Davis said with great expectancy in his eyes as he clamped down on the dead cigarillo between his thin lips. ''And then—''

''And then?''

''Cuba, my boy. And the real war.''

Richard Harding Davis sounded like he knew what he was talking about. As well he did. He was one of the very few newspapermen covering this Cuban conflict who had ever seen actual warfare—as he certainly had during the battle between Turkey and Greece, which he had reported for the London *Times*. Which was why William Randolph Hearst had hired his services this time around.

The carriage clattered back toward the town proper, the two privates still harmonizing beautifully, the horses seeming to clip-clop their hooves in some strange counterpoint. It was soothing.

''This is very strange, Dick,'' Brian said suddenly.

''What is?''

''I feel very much like another drink.''

''Not strange at all, dear novice. Hair of the dog that bit you, as they say in higher circles. It's quite the thing, you know.''

''Then can we have a toast before we leave today?''

''Trust me,'' Richard Harding Davis winked

broadly. "I have a bottle of the best in my traveling bag."

Dawn light poked long, grey fingers on the eastern horizon.

A bugle sounded faintly in the distance.

Privates Cassidy and Simpson, without dropping a note, set the horses at the gallop. The carriage rocketed forward, gathering speed.

Trained soldiers, no matter where they are, always respond to the voice of the bugle, as they do, too, to the roll of drums.

They were sounds that, once instilled in a man, can never be forgotten. Not until death comes as the end of all things.

Brian Dexter Cook sensed that now as he never had before as the horse-drawn carriage raced back from the sleazy neighborhood of the *cantina* to where it had come from. The animals snorted.

It was as if the horses were racing the dawn light.

The planned invasion of Cuba was definitely on the agenda of all things military for the United States Army. Tampa, Florida, had been selected as one of the major marshaling points. So it was that Richard Harding Davis, Brian Dexter Cook, Lois Weatherall, and literally hundreds of other reporters from papers all around the country found themselves traveling with the soldiers toward the ultimate outcome of this war. But the newest and most important step was Tampa, where they would join the expeditionary force evolved by General William R. Shafter with the help of his hard-working staff of junior officers. Among these was a first lieutenant named John J. Pershing, who already was making a reputation for himself as an officer to watch.

But the present miracle was Tampa itself.

Almost overnight, with the trainloads debarking hordes of soldiers and army materiel, Tampa became a veritable tent city. Every patch of available earth held a tent. White tents blossomed all over as the regular army men and volunteers flooded the landscape. White men, and black men, too—men who had fought in the Civil War and the Indian campaigns of the Southwest and the plains; men who knew the sound of gunfire, the flash of a sabre, the cries of the wounded and dying. And of all these, no regiment drew more attention than the First Volunteer Cavalry. This bizarre assortment, now under the full leadership of the dynamic Lieutenant Colonel Theodore Roosevelt, grew and grew until it numbered a thousand men. To the ranks of Roosevelt's boys, those hardened customers such as Tex Whitover, Hank Slocum, Bart Cody, Old Doc Hawkins, Chesterton, Peabody, and Indian Joe Jones were added adventurous Eastern college students, society playboys, and more cowboys from every corner of the United States. Two striking newcomers, one from the New York Volunteers, the other from Pennsylvania, were Louis Shepherd Stone and Big John Jameson. Stone was a young man of twenty summers with an amazing head of prematurely grey hair. His fine, resonant voice clearly indicated the actor he had been on the New York stage. Jameson was fully six feet five inches tall, as burly as a sequoia, and had been a farmer until the war broke out. These were the sort of contrasting men who felt drawn to an outfit such as Roosevelt's First Volunteer Cavalry. And long before their feet would touch Cuban soil, all the reporters in Tampa had made the country well aware of the Rough Riders. They had already become household words. Teddy's Boys.

And as training increased in intensity and the army prepared for the invasion that would come very soon, many other events were transpiring. Like ripples in the water when a pebble is tossed in.

A communiqué came from the White House, from President William McKinley himself, offering Richard Harding Davis a captaincy in the Army. Davis refused, after some consideration. His newspaperman's instinct told him to stick close by Roosevelt's new fighting unit. He was certain they would be where the action was—this despite the fact that he and the colonel were not the best of friends. Roosevelt privately regarded Dick Davis as a partying clubman who wrote his copy while sitting in saloons imbibing liquor. He felt that

Davis would "shrink from the fighting" and act like a "mollycoddle" when the chips were down. Richard Harding Davis was to prove Teddy Roosevelt dead wrong about that.

Miss Lois Weatherall tried many times to seek out Brian Dexter Cook, but he avoided her as if she carried the plague. His night with Rita Sanchez had given Brian a rather different perspective on the female kind—and besides, Miss Weatherall irritated him no end. She was a constant reminder of New York and what a fool she had made of him. He had no memory, of course of how he had murmured her name as he made passionate love to another woman.

Rita Sanchez and her secret colleagues were not idle, not by any means. She, too, left Jacksonville and took a train to Tampa where she set herself up in a room above another *cantina*. This one was called Ricardo's and was a favorite drinking place for the *soldatos* after the camp bugle blew retreat. There were women in Ricardo's. Bar women, prostitutes and lonely women gathered there, all eager to help a soldier spend his pay. No war is any different; no soldier is any different. It had been so since the beginning of time. Rita knew that, but also she knew that she could ply her spying trade much better where the troops were stationed. One never knew what vital bit of information one could pick up. There were always ways of getting such information over to Cuba—by letter or boat or even messenger.

Sergeant Dutch Henry Harkness, with a score to settle with Brian Dexter Cook and trying to find the time and place to do it, still had enough interest in Miss Lois Weatherall to send her a bunch of posies, a box of candy, and other little tokens of his esteem. Lois ignored them all as politely as possible, but she would never want to be alone with the ramrod-straight sergeant. The plain lust in the frosty blue eyes was a bit too hard to take. She had a difficult time keeping her temper and composure when he looked at her like that.

Brian Dexter Cook did not avoid Sergeant Harkness. They were bound to meet again, and when they did, both men handled the confrontation with admirable calm and restraint. The encounter came on a truly hot June afternoon with the First Volunteer Cavalry, Colonel Roosevelt at its head, practicing full charges up a low-lying ridge of earth beyond their encampment. Brian was observing from a nearby location of advantage. He thought Dutch Henry was out there with the galloping troopers, as well he should have been, but suddenly Sergeant Dutch Henry Harkness was before him, surveying him coolly from head to foot again. The Sergeant was freshly shaved, brown from the sun, and never had he looked more formidable.

Brian tensed, ready for literally any move the man might make. But he had misjudged Harkness' presence, as the man made clear at once, even though they were alone and the nearest soldier was over fifty yards away, adjusting the stake poles of his tent.

"Stand easy, Pretty Boy. I haven't come to waltz you around."

"That's good to know, Sergeant. But may I ask what *is* on your mind this glorious afternoon?"

"You cold-decked me the last time we were introduced."

"I did. And I will again if you ever call the lady any more of your pet names."

Harkness showed his blunt, even teeth.

"No trouble there. I like Miss Lois. And I was wrong to say what I did. Ignorance is no excuse, I guess. But I do want you to know I owe you one for that sock, Mr. Cook."

Brian nodded, relieved that Harkness wasn't looking for trouble this day. It was a hot afternoon—too hot for charges on horses, too hot to write copy, too hot for anything. The Tampa sun was merciless.

"You do indeed, Sergeant. I can't quarrel with that. So I'll give you satisfaction wherever and whenever you say. It's the sporting thing, I believe. As the injured party, you have the choice of weapons, also. It's the gentleman's code of the *duello*, Sergeant Harkness."

The Sergeant frowned. He placed both hands defiantly on his hips. "You funning with me,

Pretty Boy? Well, don't. I'm not talking about any duels. I just want you to know when the time comes, I'm coming at you. That's all. Just wanted you to know. I figure maybe Cuba is the spot to call you down. What with all the shooting going on.''

"That suits me just fine. Anything you say.''

"Done, then. See you around, *Mister* Cook.''

Brian Dexter Cook stared a long time as the tall figure of Dutch Henry Harkness about-faced and strode purposefully off somewhere. Brian shook his head—the war be hanged.

He had his own private war on his hands. A lulu.

And the ''other side,'' the enemy, was Sergeant Dutch Henry Harkness, clearly no lightweight by any means. Nor a buttercup or a daisy.

Just this once, in the matter of Miss Lois Weatherall and ladies in general, he dearly wished he had minded his own business.

Being a gentleman, or behaving like one, could sometimes be a very foolish, dangerous thing.

As it decidedly was *now*.

Dutch Henry was out to get him.

And then, as the very first week of June drew to a close, the universe of the tent cities was gripped with a fever of excitement, a whirlwind of activity, and the suspense and tension of preparation heightened into an almost maddening maelstrom of men, horses, and military vehicles. The orders had come.

Dawn of the seventh of June would initiate the departure of the Army, the Navy and the Marines for Cuba. The hour had come for action. Embarkation was here at last.

Major General William R. Shafter and Major General Joseph Wheeler, both Civil War veterans, coordinated their plans. Shafter was the overall commander of the proposed expeditionary force, but Wheeler would be the one on command for the land operation when the troops touched Cuban soil. Gunboats and battleships lay off the Tampa coastline, waiting and ready. Colonel Roosevelt and his Rough Riders bristled with impatience and paid extra-special attention to their weapons and their mounts. Their time had come. Roosevelt felt it in his bones, and when the final orders came, his private tent reverberated with his catchword: "Bully!" And then "Bully!" again.

To a man, the First Volunteer Cavalry could not agree with him more. Now was the hour of the truth of all things, great and small. Cuba would be the testing ground for America in matters beyond the limits of the forty-five states and the Southwest territories of Texas, New Mexico, and Oklahoma. The firing line, indeed.

But before the orders came, hours before decision, Tampa yet saw an army at play—trained men having one last blow-out before they would all be gone in the next two days. The restaurants and the bars and other areas of entertainment to be found in the city became veritable meccas. And foremost among these was Ricardo's, the Spanish-style bar of potted plants, cane chairs, and easy female company. There whiskey was cheap and the music and the lights were low.

There Rita Sanchez worked—as a spy for the government of Cuba.

The *World*'s Stephen Crane was assigned to a gunboat carrying six hundred U.S. Marines. The *Journal*'s Richard Harding Davis and the *Herald*'s Brian Dexter Cook were slated to accompany the First Volunteer Regiment on its designated vessel. Miss Lois Weatherall, despite all the telephone calls and political interference of William Randolph Hearst, was not to be allowed on any ship carrying the military to Cuba. *No matter what*— the Government was adamant.

No woman, other than service people, such as nurses, were permitted in an area where hostilities were under way. Females were not to be tolerated under any conditions. Enough was enough. Writing about the Spanish-American War from America was one thing. Writing about it from the battlefield was another. Weatherall would have to stay behind—whether she liked it or not, whether Hearst liked it or not. There were some mountains even a Hearst could not move. This surely was one of them. Nellie Bly's heroic reputation was safe.

Brian Dexter Cook was privately elated about this turn of events.

He didn't want Lois Weatherall to get hurt, not in any way.

No matter how she had betrayed him.

He was enormously grateful that Jezebel would have to stay behind. With her beautiful porcelain look, her tilted chin, and all her determined charm. She would only be in the way.

Enough was decidedly enough.


Stephen Crane did not go to Ricardo's on that last night.

He remained behind in his billet in camp.

He was suffering another sudden attack of the miserable dysentery he had picked up in Athens, Greece. The food of the local restaurants had only heightened and aggravated his stomach trouble. It would not go away.

By the light of a solitary candle, Crane tried to read to ease his torment. He was not too successful. The agony in his abdomen was enormous. He lay shivering on his cot, with his eyes closed and his mind a seething field of doubt. He was truly beginning to think he would not be able to handle Cuba and the coming battles.

He had always envied Richard Harding Davis— his dash, his vigor, his aplomb—qualities that young Brian Dexter Cook seemed to possess also, in abundance. Cook had all the tools for success in Crane's estimation. He would go far if he was not killed in Cuba.

In his agony, Stephen Crane smiled philosophically.

He had always wondered what it would be like to be shot. To suffer a wound. To endure all those things he had written so deeply and sincerely about in *The Red Badge of Courage*. When he was very young.

Courage.

Stephen Crane did not know whether he possessed it or not.

Knifing pain shot up through his stomach and he moaned.

Low, very low—so that no one could hear him.

From outside the tent, a bugle call pierced the stillness of the camp. Nine o'clock: lights-out time for military men.

At least it was lights-out for those who had stayed behind and not gone into town to carouse and ripsnort and have that one last high time before embarkation hour. Stephen Crane extinguished his candle and drew his woolen army blanket over his shivering form.

It was a warm June night, but he was cold. Colder than the tomb.

The pitch blackness of the tent made him feel worse than ever. And the pain was multiplied by the doubts and the nagging uncertainty.

Could he make it as a battlefield reporter?

Only Cuba held the answer.

\*    \*    \*

Some five miles away, in downtown Tampa, the place called Ricardo's was another kind of battlefield.

Where—as they would have said about a Clyde Fitch melodrama on Broadway—the plot was thickening.

# RICARDO'S AND RIOT

"Behold the maiden," Richard Harding Davis said. " 'She walks in beauty like the night'—and if she doesn't, she'll do until the real thing comes along." He pointed from his corner of the crowded bar. "Do you see what I see?"

Brian Dexter Cook turned, feeling relaxed and at ease, and followed the extended forefinger. Along its line, he saw Rita Sanchez coming toward them, a vision half-remembered but altogether enticing. The jet-black hair, the wide red mouth, the piercing dark eyes, the hourglass figure so amply endowed and trapped within the confines of a peasant girl blouse and a skirt whose sheer, form-fitting lines were entirely uncommon. Brian blinked, but not because of the bottle of rum that he and Dick Davis had been sharing in celebration of the morning's embarkation. Señorita Sanchez was smiling at him in a manner that bespoke of their mad, tumultuous night in the back room of the *cantina* in Jacksonville.

"Don't leave me alone with her, Dick," Brian murmured. "Not just yet."

"Very well. But you are insane. This lady is yours and I will be excess baggage, old man."

"All the same, please stay."

"As you wish."

There was no more time. Rita Sanchez had come between them, the dark eyes only for Brian Dexter Cook. Richard Harding Davis nodded to her in greeting and buried his smile in his glass of rum. All about them, the uproar was continuous and deafening. Army men, sailors, and marines had filled Ricardo's to overflowing. Laughter was raucous, mingling voices high, and a steady wave of bottles and glasses on trays in the hands of two swarthy *peons* whirled back and forth. An overhead fan rotated with a metallic clatter. The atmosphere was heavy with tobacco smoke and perspiration. From the rear of Ricardo's, leaning against the upright piano with its baldheaded, moustached player, stood Sergeant Dutch Henry Harkness surveying the room at large. But the frosty blue eyes, alert yet lidded, never strayed very far from Brian Dexter Cook. The sergeant was dressed in a freshly ironed uniform, his tie sharply defined, his campaign hat tugged down over his forehead. Dutch Henry looked as grim and military as a non-com in charge of a firing squad. Brian had seen him as soon as he and Dick Davis had entered, but had ignored him ever since. And now there were other things to think about.

"*Hola*, Brian," Rita Sanchez said with a catch in her throat. "It is good to see you again, *querida*."

"Hello, Rita. You remember Mr. Davis?"

"*Sí*, the good *señor* who rescued you from my uncle's *cantina*."

"*Señorita*," Dick Davis said politely and managed a curt bow.

"But what on earth are you doing here, Rita? We left you back in Jacksonville—"

She smiled, the dark eyes flashing.

"We are camp followers, Brian. My uncle and I. The business is better where the army is, as you see; we have made much money these last days— the *soldatos* are always so thirsty." Pointedly, she did not allude to the several women, daringly dressed—women who were already mingling with small knots of men along the bar. Richard Harding Davis set his empty glass down on the counter. "Hello—there's Jennings. That rascal owes me.

I've been standing him drinks all week. See you later, Brian—*buenas noches*, Rita.''

Before Brian could stop him, he was gone, lost in the crowded figures engulfing the *cantina*. Rita watched him go, approvingly.

''A clever man, that. He saw that I wanted to be with you only.''

''He doesn't miss much,'' Brian agreed, not sure of himself or his true feelings. ''Shall I buy you a drink?''

''No. But I do want you to come with me. To my room upstairs. There is something we must talk about—it is *muy importante*—and will be of much interest to a newspaper person who is going to Cuba so very soon.''

Brian frowned. ''Can't you tell me here?''

''No, it is too dangerous. There are too many ears.''

He hesitated only a moment longer. She had curved her body into his so that her warm and ample hip was pressing against him. The sultry, lovely face was just below his chin level. And he was only a man, after all. One who had had enough rum to lose some of his innate caution and reserve. He smiled and pointed to the half-empty bottle of rum.

''Shall I bring it?''

''No. It is not necessary. You will find everything you need in Rita's room—God's truth, Brian.''

There was no more to be said.

They pushed their way from the bar, Rita Sanchez leading the way. They threaded through
jostling, noisy men and found the wooden staircase leading upwards. The piano, which was add-
ing to the *cantina* clamor, sounded "Tenting
Tonight" in thumping chords. From its depths,
Sergeant Dutch Henry Harkness watched Pretty
Boy Cook and the eye-filling Rita Sanchez mount
the stairs. His slitted eyes narrowed in expressionless scrutiny. He did not stir from his position.
Brian Dexter Cook and the woman disappeared
into the top floor of the *cantina*.

At that precise moment, Miss Lois Weatherall
came through the bat's-wing doors of Ricardo's—on
the arm of Sergeant Louis Shepherd Stone, the
mere lad of twenty-one whose prematurely gray
hair made him so striking-looking. Behind them
loomed Big John Jameson. The actor and the farmer
had become very fast friends in the early days of
their training. And both of them had yielded to Miss
Weatherall's request to see how the men of the
Army, the Navy and the Marines comported themselves away from camp. Lieutenant Colonel Theodore Roosevelt would have heartily disapproved of
Miss Weatherall's presence in Ricardo's. But with
a gentleman like Sergeant Stone and a giant like
Jameson, what harm could come to Miss Weatherall?
She was in most excellent hands.

Richard Harding Davis, collecting his drinks
from Jennings of the *Baltimore Sun*, saw Lois and

shuddered. He had also seen Brian go upstairs with Rita Sanchez. He smelled trouble, his newspaperman's nose quivering. So he kept his eyes and ears open even as he conversed with Jennings, a tall, thin, older man with long sideburns and handlebar moustache. And at the piano, Sergeant Dutch Henry Harkness came alive.

He, too, had spotted Miss Weatherall. A grim smile eclipsed his tanned, smooth face. His smile was a Death's head.

Ricardo's might prove more interesting than even he had planned for. He moved toward Sergeant Stone, Private Jameson, and the lady, pushing a path for himself through the milling customers. His frosty blue eyes had never seemed bluer. Sergeant Harkness was very happy.

Pretty Boy Cook had cut his own throat going upstairs with a *cantina* woman. Harkness intended that would be no secret to be kept. Miss Weatherall was going to know as soon as Harkness could tell her. Dutch Henry knew men. And gentleman or no gentleman, punch or no punch, he was fully aware that this was not just any lady to Brian Dexter Cook. This was the woman he wanted, no matter what he said.

Harkness wanted her, too.

And by Christ, he was going to get her before this night ended.

A woman who can't go to Cuba can't follow you.

Sergeant Stone and Private Jameson saw him coming before Lois Weatherall did. Their faces fell. Sergeant Harkness smiled. The smile had no humor at all in it, and he came to a military stop before all three of them. It was then that Lois saw him, and her face tightened.

"Evenin', boys," Sergeant Harkness said flatly. "Mighty nice of you to deliver Miss Weatherall to me like this. I'd be privileged to take over for you now. Privileged, indeed."

A bottle smashed on the floor somewhere in Ricardo's and a woman's voice cried out in anger and a man bellowed in pain.

From those sounds forward, Ricardo's was a battleground.

Bedlam reigned.


Rita Sanchez's room was less disreputable-looking than the one Brian Dexter Cook remembered from Jacksonville. What he could remember, that is. There was one window, the shade drawn, a low bed with brass posters and a thick quilt of outlandish design and color, and one cane chair. A white-painted dresser showing chip marks and some scratches shone in the glare of a kerosene lamp. This stood on a night table by the bed. There was no carpet, merely floorboards recently washed or scrubbed. A white pitcher and a tall glass stood on the dresser. There was a postcard jutting from one corner of the oval mirror above the dresser. Brian glanced at it briefly, as he followed Rita Sanchez into the room. He closed the door and stared at her, for she had turned in the center of the room and removed several thick rings from her very strong-looking fingers. He had not noticed the rings before. Rita set them down very carefully on the night table beside the lamp. She looked back at him and her smile was long, slow, and very appealing. Her white teeth gleamed in the light of the kerosene lamp.

"Oh, Brian, it does Rita's heart good to see you."

"What did you want to talk to me about?"

"Do you not know? Can you not guess?"

He shook his head, smiling. "No," he said simply, refusing to take the obvious road. "We're alone now. Tell me."

She came toward him, extending her arms. He did not retreat.

Her arms encircled him and she buried her head against his chest. "*Querida*, I cannot bear to lose you. You are going away—when? There are so many ships—I must know—"

He sighed, feeling her warm, full body against him. Again, her magic was transmitting itself to him. Her closeness, the aromatic scent of fresh-cut flowers—he reached down and turned her face toward his own. From inches away, the lush red mouth beckoned; the dark eyes widened. He saw the look in those eyes. The naked, yearning desire.

He responded, as he had once before. Her molten mouth met his as it descended.

The kiss was fiery, volcanic, overwhelming.

Before he could gauge his own emotions or reactions, she had led him toward the low, lumpy bed with its flamboyant quilt. Her fingers were plucking at his shirt and tie, then straying to his belt buckle. Her plan was very straightforward and simple. Make love to this golden man first; then ask the questions when his guard was down, when he would not be so suspicious. She was convinced that newspaper person that he was, he must know some details of troop movements, where the ships might dock—valuable information for all the friends in Cuba. For which she would be amply rewarded.

Her plan was a good one. Brian Dexter Cook did know many things about the embarkation, and since it would take all the ships a good four to five days to reach Cuba, there would be time for Cuban forces to prepare, once they knew. But Rita Sanchez had not counted on Fate and the unexpected.

"Rita, Rita . . . you fiery little wanton . . ."

"*Sí*—for you—and only you, Brian *querida* . . ."

"The door is unlocked."

"Then I shall lock it—we will not be disturbed."

She moved toward the door, the peasant blouse already discarded. The gleaming flesh of her curved back and the superb swell of her bosom enchanted him. She clicked the door shut and turned. Her eyes slowly roved over him as she approached the bed, her fingers working on the waistband of the skin-tight skirt. When it fell away, Brian Dexter Cook felt his heart thunder in his body. She was female incarnate, and the dusky contours of her form could have graced any museum in existence. All thoughts of Lois Weatherall fled—this was Rita Sanchez.

He half rose from the bed to meet her.

She lowered herself to him. He took her in his hungry arms. Again, her flesh scalded him; the wholly wanton, pagan expression in her dark eyes ignited him. They locked and tumbled, rolling to the counterpane. And in frenzied moments, he was at her as he had been that last time. Only now he was not intoxicated, not half-insensible. Now he knew what he was doing, knew what he wanted. And he wanted this dark Spanish flower. This woman who was blood relation to those whom the United States was fighting. It did not matter now—it might never matter.

But as she widened below him to receive him, with the room all askew with flashing impressions and dizzying images, beneath the very bed on which they reveled came the sounds of trouble. The hoarse shouting of men, the shrieking voices of women, the crashing uproar of glass and wooden furniture breaking. And the almost paralyzing tumult of a gun going off—shots cannonading. The bed on which they lay seemed to rock, the floor to tremble. But not from their mutual passion.

Ricardo's was in an uproar, an explosion of noises.

No one can make love, or even think of it, when the world all about one is going up in smoke. Neither Brian nor Rita was an exception.

They froze in their naked positions. Their glances locked in the half-light. Brian Dexter Cook moved. Quickly. He reached for his clothes. Rita Sanchez did not stop him. She couldn't.

They had to find out what was going on downstairs in Ricardo's.

It sounded like the world was coming to an end all at once, in a crescendo of disaster.


The mad scene below in the bar had had a seemingly innocuous beginning—which rapidly advanced to chaos.

A Marine corporal who had had far too much *vino* had taken a fancy to a saloon woman who was shining her charms on a volunteer for the First Cavalry. The corporal had been obnoxious and abusive and picked on the Rough Rider, a gangling private from Texas. The woman had rushed to her amour's defense by crashing a whiskey bottle over the corporal's head. From that point onward, the private affair degenerated into a free-for-all which included nearly everyone in Ricardo's. The battle lines had been drawn. And even though all the participants belonged to the same army, the branches of service showed their teeth. Marines fought with Army regulars; Navy men tangled with the First Volunteer Cavalry Regiment. And no one was safe. Not even Dutch Henry Harkness, Sergeant Stone, Private Big John Jameson, and least of all, Miss Lois Weatherall. Chairs flew, tables overturned, bottles sailed, glasses were flung, and Ricardo's was the setting for a small war. The Military Police would never respond in time to save bloody noses, broken arms, or twisted necks. Pandemonium was the order of the evening.

Sergeant Harkness did himself proud. Blocking Miss Weatherall from a flying chair, he took a stance and held his ground, shooting hard-handed punches into the faces and jaws of those unwise enough to assault him. Lois shrank behind him as Stone and Jameson rallied to Harkness' flanks. Protected by the three of them, Lois was as safe as if she had been in church. Big John Jameson's six feet seven inches of height was a veritable wall of flesh which no man could get by. The gentlemanly gray-haired young Stone displayed an admirable amount of fancy footwork and deft boxing maneuvers. Harkness had no finesse, merely brute force, but it was enough. Bodies began to pile up on Ricardo's floor. And then some crazed idiot pulled a gun from somewhere and the Pier Six Brawl turned into a slaughterhouse.

A battered Marine private who had not left his weapon in camp, as he should have, went berserk and began blasting away at friend and foe alike.

The pistol shots worked wonders. Everyone scattered like leaves in a windstorm. Sergeant Harkness pulled Lois Weatherall to the floor, made a barricade of an overturned round table, and signaled Stone and Jameson to do likewise. Which they did. But the Marine private's rash act triggered a reflex action in yet another Marine. He, too, drew a pistol and fired. Ricardo's echoed with gunfire. No one had been hit as yet, but the moment was hazardous and ironic. Imagine getting wounded in a *cantina* in Tampa before the real war started in Cuba! Dick Davis and Jennings were under a table, too.

Lois Weatherall tugged at Sergeant Harkness' strong arm.

"Oh, please, can't you make them stop—this is madness!"

"It's the service, Miss Lois. Bound to happen when troops get liquored up and there's women to fight over."

"But it's so awful! Those men will kill somebody."

"They'll be out of shells soon enough, and then we'll rush them. Ready, Stone? Ready, Jameson?"

Both men on his flanks nodded eagerly, almost smiling, but both they and Sergeant Harkness had miscalculated. Also, they had not counted on Brian Dexter Cook coming on the dead-run down the steps from the floor above—with Rita Sanchez breathlessly at his heels.

From that moment forward, there was no accounting for how it happened. The tragedy. The calamity. There were scores of eyewitnesses, but not even the Marine private could have said why he fired toward the stairs and the two figures flashing down its steps. The man and the woman. That newspaper fellow and the dame who worked in Ricardo's.

The final shell in the private's pistol went off. And then came the click of the hammer falling on an empty chamber. But between the blast of gunfire and the following click, everyone saw the terrible tableau on the stairs leading down from the top floor.

Rita Sanchez let out a startled bleat of sound, no more than a half-choked cry. A look of incredible surprise and shock fixed her beautiful face into a frieze of horror. Nobody could see the ugly hole that abruptly appeared directly over the bodice of her bosom. For she was falling, her arms outflung. Brian Dexter Cook was well ahead of her, coming down those stairs, but she reached the bottom long before him—bouncing, rolling, thumping, until her shapely figure landed in a grotesque, contorted heap at the base of the stairs. Brian halted in disbelief.

The *cantina* went as still as death. As quiet as a funeral parlor.

No one said a word for a full few seconds. Only

the clattering whir of the overhead fan could be heard.

And then Lois Weatherall put her hands to her face and screamed.

Only then did everyone move—pulled from their shock, their paralysis of action and movement.

Brian Dexter Cook reached Rita Sanchez first.

Knowing he would dread what he found.

She had died before she reached the last step of the staircase.

The random shot had struck home, directly into the heart—a killing strike.

"Good, merciful God," Brian Dexter Cook almost whispered. "She's dead."

No one could disagree with that, either.


"I'd court-martial the lot of them," Colonel Theodore Roosevelt roared to Commanding Officer Leonard Wood in the privacy of the huge pyramidal tent with its packed equipment and stored-away maps and battle plans. "Troops have a right to kick up their heels—relieves tension and all that—but by thunder, reckless shooting of firearms I'll not tolerate. If it weren't that we were shoving off in two hours, I'd make an inquiry all down the line. Still, it is the hand of the Almighty and a blessing in disguise."

Colonel Wood nodded somberly. "Who else was aware that this Sanchez woman was a Cuban spy?"

"No one, Colonel. Save myself and the military police assigned to watch that trouble spot. Perhaps it's all for the best. We hardly have time for a trial."

Outside, with the first light of dawn breaking once more over Tampa, the campsite was alive with activity. The sounds of men, horses, and equipment readying for the long march to the docks where the gunboats and warships yet lay at anchor. It was a hubbub that excited Teddy Roosevelt. He and the men, the Rough Riders in particular, had waited far too long for this day. It had only been two months, but it now seemed like years.

"Thank God, Miss Weatherall was not hurt. That would have created a furor, wouldn't it? Hearst's lady reporter injured in a barroom scuffle with military personnel. I shudder to think of it."

Wood shook his head and eyed T.R. fondly.

"You old walrus. This incident merely underscores how correct the United States government is in not allowing her to go to Cuba with us. Don't you agree?"

"Absolutely—I never quarreled with that decision. Though Miss Weatherall is pleasing at all times to the eye. Bully for Harkness and Stone and Big John for getting her out of that *cantina* before the military police arrived. That would have been sticky, but these Riders of mine are cool in the face of difficulties. It will stand them in good stead in Cuba."

His superior was buckling on his tunic and cartridge belt and holstered horse pistol. Roosevelt eyed him with approval. Wood would be a fine man in the coming campaign. He sensed it in his very bones.

"Colonel Wood?"

"Yes, T.R.?"

"Bully being with you on this thing—bully, indeed."

Colonel Leonard Wood smiled wearily. He extended a hand.

"Let us hope we both have a good outing in Cuba."

"Amen to that, sir." Roosevelt shook that hand warmly, firmly.

Somewhere outside came the pealing call of "Boots and Saddles."

Colonel Theodore Roosevelt's eyes glittered behind his rimless glasses. The Rough Riders were hitting the leather. Getting ready to ride. Off to Cuba, off to glory, off to the great unknown.

By God, thought Teddy Roosevelt, whatever's waiting for us across the waters, we'll be ready for it.

And every man will do his duty, as sure as there is a God in the blue heavens. They were all Americans and would not shirk from their responsibilities as men and soldiers. And patriots.

It was June seventh, eighteen hundred and ninety-eight.

The first American troops were ready to go to Cuba, ready to free the Cuban people from the yoke of Spanish tyranny.

Dewey was holding the blockade at Manila Bay and Admiral Sampson was closing in on Cervera with his North Atlantic Fleet. The very next move was to send the men in to take the ground on the flanks, away from the Spanish fort guns ringing all the harbors—particularly at Santiago de Cuba, which was the point where General William R. Shafter was going to center his invasion forces. God willing, no later than next week.

The bugle continued to peal long, clear, trumpeting notes.

It was a lovely sound, from any standpoint.

Brian Dexter Cook knew he had to say goodbye to Lois Weatherall, despite all his inner torment with her and his guilty feelings about Rita Sanchez's death. During all the commotion and stunned reactions to the Spanish woman's death, he had not been blind to Lois' presence. Nor did he miss the withering glare she gave him as he crouched so forlornly over Rita Sanchez's body. Seeing her with Dutch Henry Harkness was the crowning indignity. Watching Harkness and a pair of First Cavalry Volunteers hurry her out of Ricardo's merely depressed him even more. And then Dick Davis rushed to his side and all the questions and confusions mounted. The chastened combatants, the Army, the Navy, and the Marines, had all closed in on the hapless private with the gun and held him until the police arrived. After that, it was all nightmare and more perplexing hours.

Until it was dawn and the embarkation of some fifteen thousand troops was under way. And Dick Davis helped him through the bewilderment of packing to get ready for going board ship with the First Volunteer Cavalry. Dick was sympathetic, as usual, but carefully packed his own field glasses, white collars, felt hats, and field boots. He would go to Cuba in Richard Harding Davis style. It did not matter what any other reporter wore or did. And he fully intended to go with the first boats. Brian Dexter Cook almost did not care anymore. He was a very befuddled young man. Until he made up his mind to seek out Lois Weatherall and bid her good-bye, as a man. Not as a weak-kneed sophomore newsman.

"I've got to say good-bye to her before we shove off, Dick. You can see that, can't you?"

"Of course, you've got to, you young fool. I can also see something else. Something all too apparent from the beginning."

"What do you mean?"

"You still love her, Brian. No matter what she did to you. Why not get that out in the open and stop torturing yourself. She's quite a woman, you know. Pity she loves you. I'd go for her myself."

"Love me? You're insane. She was only doing a job for Hearst."

"If you still think that's all it was, then I'm sorry for you, dear Mr. Cook." Richard Harding Davis held up the field glasses. "These are really rum, you know. Picks up everything over five hundred feet away. When I was in Greece—"

Brian Dexter Cook did not hear the rest of that. He had already left the room, going off in search of Miss Lois Weatherall.

Before there was no more time left to say good-bye.

Unfortunately for all concerned, Sergeant Dutch Henry Harkness wanted to make his farewells to Miss Lois Weatherall, too. He reached her long before Brian Dexter Cook did. Grateful to him for his help the night before, Lois let the Sergeant into her room. Harkness, as cunning and resourceful as any wolf stalking a lamb, immediately launched himself at Lois when she turned away to check the tiny watch lying on her night table. The sergeant had closed in on her and, with a powerful, mashing embrace, crushed her in his arms as he forced his lips down on her mouth. She was no match for him and Dutch Henry literally vised her in his grasp. She could not even twist her head out of the way or scream, as she desperately wanted to. "Miss Lois, honey—"

So it was that Brian Dexter Cook entered the

room and saw the woman of his dreams locked in a long kiss with the man he hated; there was little for him to do but turn away and leave as quietly as he had come. So it was, too, that he missed entirely what happened when the sergeant released the lady and stepped back with a crooked grin on his cruel, taut face. The resounding slap delivered from the heels nearly rocked Dutch Henry's head from his shoulders. It was a stinging reprimand.

"Get out," Lois Weatherall hissed, her lovely face deathly white, "before I scream and have you horse-whipped."

Sergeant Dutch Henry Harkness knew she meant what she said.

Shrugging, he tipped his hat to her, saluted softly, and withdrew.

Down below, somewhere in the vicinity of his own room, Brian Dexter Cook, face inflamed with rage and inner heart twisted with anger and hurt, stalked grimly away from the woman who continued to make such a fool of him. The damn hussy—practicing her wiles on everybody in pants—what wouldn't she do to get a story or get on board the ship that the government had refused her.

Miss Lois Weatherall, the perfect Hearst reporter.

Brian Dexter Cook's handsome face contorted in a snarl.

He couldn't wait to get to Cuba fast enough.

Women. *Pah*.

Wars were far easier to understand than they would ever be.

Damn them all. Every sweet-faced, lying mother's daughter of them.

Wenches, wantons, *trollops* . . .

Brian Dexter Cook swallowed the word. It was distasteful to him.

He had never been more miserable in his life. Not ever.

And in far-off Cuba, perhaps death was waiting for him, too.

Death, at least, was a man.

Not a lying, deceitful, beautiful woman.

With a face like an angel come down to Earth . . .

There was still one more disappointment in Tampa. Brian was not to get off or out without losing something else besides Miss Lois Weatherall. When he threw his gear together in the tent he shared with Richard Harding Davis in camp, it was only to find a glaring loss. The valuable Bausch & Lomb telescope was missing. It was nowhere to be found. Search as he might, both high and low, the prized souvenir of his Cornell days was gone. Possibly, forever.

It was inconceivable that Dick Davis had taken it. And he had not. The truth of the matter was that military men have many thieves in their ranks— those who would steal a comrade's possessions if it were worth enough to raise the price of a drink or an evening in town. Brian was bitterly upset that a Rough Rider might be a cheap and ordinary thief, but there it was—the telescope could not have gotten up and walked out of the steamer trunk. And it hadn't.

Sergeant Dutch Henry Harkness had scored but one more coup on his rival. He'd rifled the trunk while Brian was off somewhere and then pawned the telescope in a Tampa store for not even one-tenth of what it was worth. The sergeant did not care. He would steal anything from Brian Dexter Cook that he knew Pretty Boy valued. The telescope certainly had been one of those things. He had heard Brian talk enough about it during their stay in the tent city. Harkness had merely waited for the right opportunity to make his stealthy move.

So he had gone one-up on Pretty Boy Cook again.

He fully intended to do a great deal more before they finished up this Cuban campaign. There would be lots and lots of chances to cut Brian Dexter Cook down to size. If there weren't, Sergeant Harkness was determined to create them. Miss Weatherall was merely icing on the cake. He had little trouble remembering how warm and nice her mouth felt when he'd kissed her. The slap was something else again.

Damn, but she still would be worth fighting for. Not even that Sanchez female was in her class. Too bad she wasn't going to Cuba.

What a time he could have had with her under the palm trees.

Sergeant Harkness, like Brian Dexter Cook, could not know that Miss Lois Weatherall was still not to be counted out of Cuba.

She wasn't going to quit without a fight.

# SANTIAGO AND SPANIARDS

In that vital second week of June, America and the world waited with bated breath, knowing that the Expeditionary Force was on its way to blockaded Cuba. Dewey still held Havana with his six warships. Sampson was watch-dogging Cervera and the Spanish fleet in the landlocked harbor of Santiago de Cuba.

And it was here that a Naval captain named John Woodward Philip gave a new meaning to decency and grace in combat. As his ship's guns raked a Spanish vessel and sent if flaming to the bottom of the bay, and his men stood along the railing, lustily cheering their victory, Captain Philip cried out, "Don't cheer, boys. Those poor devils are dying . . ."

The Asiatic and North Atlantic Fleets of the United States Navy had done their job and done it all too well. Now it only remained for the land forces, the ground troops, to move in. Major General William R. Shafter's plan was under way. His Civil War colleague, Major General Joseph Wheeler, was in full agreement with the strategy to take Santiago.

"Assault Santiago by land," was the military directive.

It was to be obeyed to the letter. And the hour.

But on June tenth, one of the first gunboats touched on Cuban shores. It landed on the eastern shore of Guantanamo Bay, below Santiago. This vessel held some six hundred battle-eager U.S. Marines and civilian reporters. Stephen Crane, still in pain, was among them.

Sailing through the Gulf of Mexico and swinging around to the Caribbean Sea, Crane's gunboat slipped to the furthermost tip of the island. There, the Marines debarked to find the tropical-green landscape of a country centuries old. A fourth of the island was covered with mountains and hills. Rolling plains, gentle slopes, and wide, fertile valleys dominated the rest of the terrain. There were whole sections of impenetrable cane, palm-tree-lined acreage, and more than two hundred rivers and streams, most of them too short and too shallow for any kind of reasonable navigation. But the Marines had come to stay, so they dug in. It was the rainy season for Cuba and a fine light mist filled the air. Six hundred men prepared for the enemy with tents and alert sentinels and a camp perimeter of enormous size.

And then the first shots came.

Sporadic fire from the low-lying hills that lay before them. Guerilla snipers were badgering the newcomers. The Marines returned the fire with a vengeance, enjoying their very first taste of combat in this war. Ill and nervous, Stephen Crane carried dozens of filled canteens back and forth to the men positioned on the low hilltops who were accommodating the Spanish guerillas. The Cuban land war had begun. The Navy was to take a back seat now.

Stephen Crane felt the first onslaught of fever. He was trembling visibly that first night and devoured quinine pills as if they were candy. The sharpshooters continued to fire away at the dug-in Marines from a crude blockhouse in the hills.

Four days later, the Marines thundered into the jungle undergrowth, driving the guerillas from their position. Stephen Crane was still with them and getting sicker by the hour. But he refused all offers to leave the field of battle. He was determined to carry on.

To find his own red badge of courage.

And on June twenty-second, Major General William R. Shafter began his long-planned operation. Over fifteen thousand troops put their feet down on the Cuban earth. At Daiquirí and Siboney, little coastal towns near Santiago, from which Shafter envisioned a two-pronged assault against the city, the troops were landed and deployed with little resistance offered by the Spanish forces. Wood and Roosevelt's Rough Riders were among the first troops to come ashore. And Richard Harding Davis and Brian Dexter Cook and Jennings and all the rest of the reporters gleefully sent their dispatches to their newspapers. And America and the world rejoiced. The Army and the Marines were in Cuba, now! Victory could not be very far away— and the Rough Rider Regiment had already become a national treasure in which Americans could take pride and joy.

With the best yet to come.

American patrols scoured the woods beyond the beaches of Daiquirí and Siboney, rooting out Spanish sharpshooters and guerillas who tried to plague them as they fell back. And reconnaissance troops of Shafter's forces reported a stone fort at El Caney which a small Spanish force was strongly defending. Before this military objective so vital to a takeover of Cuba lay the main Spanish defenses of Kettle

Hill and San Juan Hill. Truly, a cavalry operation, to take those hills while the main body of Shafter's command pushed onward to El Caney and its heavily defended fort.

A job for the Rough Riders, clearly.

Then came the occurrence that electrified the newspaper-reading universe. An American act of courage, individuality, and soldiering that defied all adjectives. With U.S. forces holding the beaches of Daiquirí and Siboney, word had to be sent to the Cuban army holed up in the woods some two miles north of Santiago, behind the enemy guns. General Calixto Garcia y Iñiquez had to be informed of the military situation in Cuba now that the United States had landed. Garcia would also have to be asked what help he needed to coordinate his battle plans with the *Americanos*. It was absolutely necessary to victory in Cuba that this be done. To thoroughly checkmate Spanish forces.

So it was that Lieutenant Andrew Summers Rowan of the United States Army, alone and traveling through totally occupied enemy territory, delivered his commanding officer's message to Garcia.

In the guise of an English sportsman and making good use of the Spanish he had learned during military service in Chile years before, Lieutenant Rowan reached the camp of General Garcia and delivered the message. Through swamps, thick jungle, and confusing terrain, the doughty Rowan found his man. And the world gasped with incredulity and applauded an American who had performed an act above and beyond the call of duty. Lieutenant Andrew Summers Rowan had volunteered for the assignment. The message had been simple enough. *What aid do you need, General Garcia? We are here.*

They certainly were.

American land forces now held the shores of Cuba in a vise.

Havana and Santiago were still blockaded and the Expeditionary Force was in position for the total, all-out charge over the Spanish mainland. And now there was nothing for the world to do but wait.

To scout the route of march to Santiago, a U.S. infantry brigade moved southward to the village of Siboney. Major General Wheeler, in charge of the land forces, with General Shafter commanding from one of the warships in the harbor, was disgusted with the notion that infantry should be given such a job when it clearly was a cavalry operation. So, using his own interpretation and sense of the rightness of things, he sent the First Volunteer Cavalry—on foot—to circle the flank of the infantry. The Rough Riders marched toward the tiny village of Las Guasimas, where Roosevelt's trail would meet with a cavalry brigade, under the command of Major General S.B.M. Young, west of his position.

Las Guasimas was to merit full discussion in many newspaper accounts and records of this war. Brian Dexter Cook and Richard Harding Davis, refusing to stay behind as Colonel Roosevelt had ordered them to, were moving forward on foot with the troops.

Hardly suspecting they were moving into a battle royal.

On the date of June twenty-fourth, Brian Dexter Cook met history.

In the company of Dick Davis, a correspondent who had been there before. They were both carrying carbines now, on Colonel Roosevelt's explicit orders. "You damn fools," he had bristled at them before the long march. "You won't be stopping any Spaniards by pushing your pencils at them!"

Wiser words were never spoken—in or out of Cuba.

The Cuban jungle was hot, fetid, steaming, and thick with foliage and flies. Mosquitoes hummed in the oppressive air. Major General Leonard Wood was at the head of the dismounted column of Rough Riders. The going was hazardous and tough. Soldiers used their carbines to thrust aside tangled vines and dense thickets. The native vegetation was a sore problem—one that Roosevelt, a bit further back of the column in the rear with Brian Dexter Cook and Dick Davis, had discussed daily since the landing. Davis, using his valuable field glasses, had seen clear across the valley to the low-lying hills where figures of men looking as small as ants were stirring.

Never had Brian Dexter Cook missed the Bausch & Lomb telescope more. He still had no notion of where it had gone or who the thief was. At no time on the troop ship crossing the Gulf and swinging around the Caribbean had anyone come forward to own up to the theft. Dick Davis had told him to forget the whole thing—knowing the Army and its habits and customs as he did. But the persistent leer and taunting smile of Sergeant Dutch Henry Harkness all through the shipboard days had stayed with Brian. But he could not confront the man and accuse him unless he wanted another set-to. There had been no time for that. Not with this war in full swing. Harkness, a good soldier, would be needed for the coming struggle. As he was needed now. Here, in the Cuban sun, with the Rough Riders marching into Lord-knew-what.

The activity on the ridges ahead, the men moving about, the heat, the dampness had made Roosevelt's unit all tense. They were marching forward, at a half-crouch, weapons at high port. There was thunder in the air, as silent as it was. An onimous aura of something coming . . .

"What do you see out there, Dick?"

"Guerillas. Quite a bunch of them. This is going

to get pretty thick in short order, old son. Keep alert.''

"You don't have to tell me that. But thanks, just the same.''

"You're most welcome, colleague.''

They both laughed and Richard Harding Davis advanced another ten feet and dropped to the ground again, spreading some ferns before him. He leveled the field glasses once more. Up ahead, General Wheeler had halted, telling his men to fan out to the flanks. A rifle bolt clicked in the stillness of the jungle. More mosquitoes droned. Davis aimed his field glasses. Suddenly, he let out a low whistle. All at once, amazingly, he could pick out Spanish riflemen in sombreros.

When the burst of gunfire came, rifles going off in a fusillade of shots, the troops scattered, taking cover. Brian Dexter Cook hit the earth and aimed his carbine. Colonel Roosevelt, tanned and swarthy beneath his campaign hat, chuckled. "Now it begins, young gentlemen. Stay with me and try not to get killed.''

If he was jesting, it was pure irony or gallows humor. As the troopers returned the Spanish rifle fire, a soldier near Brian cried out in mortal agony. And died right before his eyes. Grimly, Brian raced to the fallen man, pulling another soldier down to cover. The exchange of shots was furious and persistent. Another trooper, off to Brian's left, dropped his carbine and toppled face-forward into a muddy ditch, his face a splash of crimson. Colonel Roosevelt swore an oath and kept on blasting away with his horse pistol. But the distance was too far for much effect. Dick Davis was still peering through his field glasses.

Colonel Roosevelt bellowed aloud for a charge. Davis lowered his glasses and raised his carbine. Brian fell in beside him. The Rough Riders, shouting and yelling, trampled through the jungle undergrowth en masse, firing as they came. Brian joined the charge, exhilarated, unafraid, his blood pounding in his veins. He lost sight of Dick Davis and T.R. Major General Wheeler, in the van, had erupted with a fierce Rebel yell. The Rough Riders broke into a clearing. Before them stood a tiny tin shack from which rifle snouts poked. The Spaniards were making their stand. Colonel Roosevelt blasted the air with a joyous shout: "The huts, men. The huts! There they are—all of them—let's rout the devils out, by God."

It was true.

Surrounding the tin fortress, a collection of concealed huts and hastily dug trenches now revealed a large body of Spaniards, all firing and reloading as fast as they could. The Rough Riders swept forward, everyone shouting and shooting. Brian Dexter Cook had never killed a man before. But he did now. Dropping a sombrero-wearing man who loomed up before him, trying to cut him in half with a vicious-looking *machete*. The fork of the trail where the huts ended and the roadway swung outward became the setting for carnage. Men screamed and died. Gunshots thundered. Major General Wheeler, so carried away with the heat of battle that he forgot for a moment what war this was, blurted: "We got the damn Yankees on the run!" Colonel Roosevelt dispatched two leaping Spaniards with a double burst of the pistol he held. His rimless glasses twinkled in the sunlight despite the dust of battle. Dick Davis was assisting a dying Yank, holding the man's head in his lap as blood streamed from his mouth. Brian Dexter Cook lowered his carbine. The dead and dying lay all around him. The remaining Spanish defenders were dropping their weapons and raising their hands. Their swarthy faces were sullen and defiant. But they knew when they were licked. These Yankee dogs had very big teeth—*sí, amigos*.

The Rough Riders surrounded their prizes, with tired, grim smiles and rueful memories of their dead comrades lying about on the steaming earth. Las Guasimas had fallen. But not without cost.

A small but very insignificant outpost on the road to Santiago.

And ultimate victory.


"Gentlemen, I am truly pleased with your behavior on the field this afternoon. *Bully*, indeed." Colonel Theodore Roosevelt, in the gathering dusk of the village of Las Guasimas had summoned

Brian Dexter Cook and Richard Harding Davis to his tent. There, by kerosene lamp, T.R. was making his feelings known. "I'm having a citation prepared for you both. With Colonel Wood's complete endorsement, I might add. No one has shown me or the Army more courage or acted in a more soldierly fashion than you two non-combatant reporters. I am proud of you. Proud to call you Americans and serve with you."

Brian and Dick exchanged sheepish glances, but they were enormously pleased. To seem right and good in the eyes of a man like T.R. was the zenith in hosannahs. But they found it difficult to speak.

"Furthermore," Roosevelt continued firmly. "I'm offering you both officer's rank in the First Volunteer Cavalry. How does that sit with you two?"

Both correspondents did not have to look at each other then, but it was Brian who replied first, remembering Dick Davis' refusal of McKinley's offer back there in May.

"Thank you, Colonel, but I must decline—great honor though it certainly is."

"You owe me your reasons, Brian. Please explain."

"I'm a reporter, sir. Equipped for the job of writing and reporting the news. I don't think I'm a leader of men going into battle."

Roosevelt nodded and swung his gaze to Richard Harding Davis.

"And you, Davis? Same reason, I suppose, since

you turned the offer down once before I recall—
from none other than the President.''

Dick Davis smiled bleakly.

"Brian said it for both of us, Colonel Roosevelt.
All I can add is 'Hear, Hear.' ''

Teddy Roosevelt snorted. "Damn fools, the pair
of you. Well, all right. But I hereby declare you
Honorary Rough Riders, and if you refuse that—by
thunder—I'll take a boot to the pair of you. Now,
get out and get back to your posts. Get some
sleep—this campaign is not over yet and tomorrow
may be rougher than today.''

Outside the tent, eavesdropping behind the flap,
Sergeant Dutch Henry Harkness, stepped quickly
back into the darkness of the jungle. Brian and
Dick Davis did not see him as they exited from
Colonel Roosevelt's command post. They strolled
back to their own tent, speaking in low tones. The
sergeant's tall figure blended with the darkness.

In the shadows, Dutch Henry pondered over
what he had heard. His thin smile was scornful
and a trifle angry.

So Pretty Boy rated a citation, did he?

Well, there was still plenty of time before that
came.

Sergeant Dutch Henry Harkness had also taken
part in the Battle of Las Guasimas, bringing up the
left flank with Stone, Jameson, Tex Whitover,
Bart Cody, and most of the cowboy bunch, the
wrangler breed.

He had killed six men himself in the heat of the day.

Without qualms, compunction, or even raising a sweat.

He was the perfect soldier for war, indeed.

An emotionless executioner. A killing machine.

As for Colonel Theodore Roosevelt, he was inordinately pleased that he could take Richard Harding Davis out of the "mollycoddle class" forever. The man had shown gumption and coolness under fire. Bully.

He had never had any doubts at all about Brian Dexter Cook.

Fine, fine young man. The cream of American manhood.

He hoped his sons would grow up to be like Brian Dexter Cook.


In their hastily written dispatches for their respective papers, Brian and Dick Davis recorded the Battle of Las Guasimas for posterity. Both correspondents, deft and facile with words, vividly recaptured the fray of that afternoon. *Journal* and *Herald* readers would cheer.

Richard Harding Davis wrote: . . .*And so, when instead of retreating on each volley, the Rough Riders rushed at them, cheering and filling the hot air with wild cowboy yells, the dismayed enemy retreated upon Santiago, where he announced he had been attacked by the entire American Army.*

Brian Dexter Cook summed it up another way: . . .*The rifles crashed; the Rebel yell of General Wheeler sounded in the warm sunshine and Colonel Theodore Roosevelt, at the head of his charging Rough Riders, secured the last bastion of Las Guasimas, driving the enemy back to Santiago. American arms had triumphed. The field was ours. . . .*

Both dispatches made the front pages of their powerful newspapers—and thrilled Americans from coast to coast. These were stirring words.

The Spanish-American War seemed under control all the way.

With men like T.R. and General Wheeler leading the troops, the United States was bound to win out in the end. Bound to.


Stephen Crane had gone with the cavalry brigade headed by Major General Young earlier that day and so had missed the entire battle action at Las Guasimas. Fortunately, perhaps. Crane was still doubled-up with dysentery cramps and could hardly stay seated on his horse. When camp was made in Siboney that night, he retired to his tent very early, swallowing quinine pills once more. His fever was worsening—something he told no one, though they could see his condition for themselves. The high fever and the morbid sense that he was a failure as both a war correspondent and a soldier continued to dog Stephen Crane.

In fact, he was heard to remark, by a fellow reporter, before he entered his tent that night: "To be shot would really be very interesting. I wonder what that feels like."

The colleague of Richard Harding Davis and Brian Dexter Cook was actually a very sick young man. Everyone was diagnosing it as yellow fever, but in truth, Stephen Crane was suffering from acute exhaustion and the multiple ills of the effects of cruel heat, ugly dampness, and that chronically upset stomach. His health was beginning a breakdown that would never end.

He would get no better on the long hard trail to Santiago.

No matter how much quinine he forced into his stomach.

He had found his red badge, but he was the last man to know that.

For he had also begun to find solace in whiskey.

He was drinking heavily on the eve of the major assault on the city of Santiago, with the Rough Riders ready to storm Kettle Hill and San Juan Hill to secure the heavily defended blockhouse there. The ring of fortified hills which lay before Santiago was crucial to the outcome of the war. Santiago would not fall if Kettle Hill and San Juan Hill were not taken and held while Colonel Garcia and his rebel army came down from the hills to the north to seal off the escape route of the Spanish army in Santiago. The back door, as it were.

Lieutenant Rowan's message to Garcia had fulfilled its meaning. Garcia and his men were ready. It only remained for the Rough Riders to swing into action. The last days of June were waning—and on the night of June thirtieth, the Rough Riders received their last-minute instructions.

They would ride on July the first.

A full-scale charge. A cavalry charge.

Into hell or to glory.

With Colonel Theodore Roosevelt on the lead horse.

T.R.—America's new Man of the Hour.


They lay in the darkness of the tent they shared, Brian Dexter Cook and Richard Harding Davis, each alone with his own thoughts, or perhaps merely listening to the sounds of the Cuban night. Some of the Rough Riders had not yet rolled into their blankets, preferring to sit around the campfire to smoke and jaw about the events of the day. And the morning battle to come. The men sounded happy and not too afraid. Someone was playing a mouth organ and someone else had raised his fine baritone in song. It was an old Irish air that Brian Dexter Cook had never heard before. Dick Davis, for all his gay banter, was deeply concerned about the woeful living conditions these troops and other U.S. servicemen had undergone. It was pitiful, really. Dysentery, yellow fever, poor Army rations—the men were not properly equipped with clothing and materiél for a jungle campaign. Cuba must have caught the Army by surprise. Living conditions were truly miserable for the men of the services. As outspoken as he was, Dick Davis was determined to make a full report to Congress and the American people when the fighting was done.

"Richard."

"How formal we are."

"Don't play the fool, please. This is serious."

"It must be. You sound so solemn."

"I suppose I am. It's just that none of us knows what tomorrow will bring."

"When do we ever? Nothing new in that, is there, Brian?"

"This isn't the same thing. We're in a battle zone. We could be killed or maimed when the Colonel takes the Riders up those hills. I saw that blockhouse on San Juan through your field glasses today. They've got more cannon—" Brian's modulated voice paused in the darkness. Dick Davis frowned at the ceiling of the tent.

"Out with it. What are you getting at, old man?"

"If something should happen tomorrow—if I should fall, and not come back—I want you to write a letter for me."

"Oh."

"Nothing long or complete with unnecessary details. It's simply that I have no family left. That I am alone in this world. I do think you could write this letter and deliver it, however you do, to Miss Weatherall back in the States.''

"And just what would the contents of this letter be?''

"Just tell her how sorry I am that things did not work out between us, that I bore her no grudge—and that—that—''

"That you love her madly, passionately, and really couldn't live without her if they gave you a crack at reincarnation? Oh, Brian, for God's sakes. When will you behave like the man and gentleman I know you to be? You're talking like a schoolboy.''

There was another long pause from the direction of Brian's cot. And then came an almost petulant rebuttal. "Am I, Dick?''

"Damn right, you are. For one thing, talk about death is gloomy nonsense. If it happens, it happens. But it is not for the likes of us, you see. For another thing, you're a writer and a good one. Why on earth should I write a letter for you? Longfellow, old man? *The Courtship of Miles Standish* and all that rot—speak for yourself, John! The sooner you own up to the simple truth that you adore Lois Weatherall, the happier you will be. And I will get some much-needed sleep. Apart from that—'' He chuckled in the darkness, his old bantering laugh.

"Apart from that? . . .'' Brian echoed foolishly, confused.

"Your lady love is not in America. She's right

here in Cuba. Or rather out there on the beach, serving with a medical detachment. She packed it in with Hearst and signed on for this war as a nurse. So forget all this letter business. Tell her in person when you see her, eh? She came over on the last ship to leave Tampa Bay. I wasn't going to tell you until the shooting ended, but this nonsense of yours has got my back up. Now, will you quiet down and go to sleep? I am tired.''

"Sleep?" raved Brian Dexter Cook, a fever of instant excitement and romantic fervor gripping him. It didn't matter what she had done to him—Lois here!—that radiant female, that wondrous girl, that darling—"How can I sleep now that you throw a bombshell like that at me?"

"Good Lord," Richard Harding Davis implored the tent and the world at large. "Is there no end to this boy's madness?"

There wasn't.

Brian Dexter Cook lay trembling in the darkness, thinking, hoping, imagining, wondering, pondering, musing over ten thousand possibilities and ten thousand ways of getting in touch with Lois Weatherall to settle the long hurt and differences between them.

He could not think about dying anymore.

Or even the next day's battle.

Nor even the betrayal in Manhattan, her working for Hearst and spying on him and that awful kiss he had seen her share with Harkness. That was all water under the bridge now.

She had abandoned Hearst, sacrificed her promising career to serve as a nurse with a war going on—and by God, he loved her for that! As he had always loved her, without even admitting it to himself. What a girl, what a woman. If only it wasn't too late to make amends. To patch things up, to seal the rift between them.

Richard Harding Davis was so right, as usual. The old master.

He loved Lois Weatherall madly, passionately, and could not live without her. That was the cold, blank-faced truth—and shame, the Devil. What was the use of pretending anymore?

No use at all, that's what.

So he lay there, Brian Dexter Cook did, on his little cot in the pitch-darkness of the tent and dreamed impossible dreams. Richard Harding Davis had fallen asleep at last.

Now was only tomorrow and San Juan Hill.

With Colonel Theodore Roosevelt and his Rough Riders.

And Destiny.

# SAN JUAN HILL AND SLAUGHTER

The morning of July 1, 1898, dawned bright and clear, but almost immediately the scorching sun and the hot, close atmosphere of the low-lying Cuban terrain made its presence felt. The air became oppressive and warm. The temperature soared. The matted vines of the jungle and the clinging foliage made advancement very awkward. But the First Volunteer Cavalry moved out, responding to the clarion call of the bugle. The Rough Riders formed in rows of threes and then wheeled in a full circle to come up behind their column commanders. And in the lead, as though he were riding point for a cavalry unit, rode Lieutenant Colonel Theodore Roosevelt. Veteran horseman that he was from nearly two decades of being a cowpoke on his Dakota ranches, T.R. was in his element. Never had he looked more formidable or impressive than he did to Brian Dexter Cook that history-making morning. There was a zest and enthusiasm to all his movements that presaged great things about to happen.

Behind him, their faces firm and expectant, rode the men of his command: men who loved him, men who would gladly die for him, and just might this very day; men of the caliber of Tex Whitover, Hank Slocum, Bart Cody, Old Doc Hawkins, Chesterton, Peabody, Indian Joe Jones, and Sergeant Louis Stone and Big John Jameson. Dutch Henry Harkness was in the saddle, also—a man who would be great to have on your side in a fight, no matter his lack of grace and manners. Etiquette was out of order on a battlefield. Nerve and straight-shooting was all that counted. Colonel Roosevelt and his Rough Riders were ready.

Brian and Dick Davis had to remind themselves that they were in the field to report, not to fight. But that was not easy to do when you put your horse in line with columns of advancing riders and you toted a carbine as they did. The Spaniards would not be able to tell one white man from another when the bullets flew and the battle smoke rose. It was best to be prepared—anything might happen.

Moving out in orderly cavalry maneuver, the Rough Riders advanced. Before them rose the twin hills of Kettle and San Juan. General William R. Shafter had timed an assault against strongly defended El Caney where a stone fort held the northern defense of Santiago. He had employed nearly half his command. The frontal assault would have to come against Kettle Hill and San Juan Hill. To this task, he had trusted Roosevelt and Wood. It was a job for the Rough Riders. The key blockhouse was on San Juan Hill. This was Colonel Roosevelt's responsibility. Wood would attack Kettle Hill, head on, with charging horses and men. There was tension in the air as the columns of riders divided, each detachment setting its horses from a trot to the gallop now. Brian and Dick Davis, riding with Colonel Teddy, were to be part and parcel of the memorable ride up those Spanish hills.

Clouds of dust lifted behind the thundering hooves of hundreds of horses. The bugle sounded the charge. Colonel Roosevelt lifted his saber to the sky and brandished it aloft as he rode. Brian and Dick Davis kept pace. The Rough Riders, campaign hats strapped to their chins, carbines and pistols flashing in the sun, hooted and hollered all the way. The Spanish blockhouse on San Juan Hill opened fire. Cannon blasted. Rifles snapped. Kettle Hill sent down a rolling salvo of gunfire. The battle was on. The overhead sky, drenched with heat and daylight mist, looked down on the tableau. The Rough Riders coming on in a sweeping horde of men and horses, the Spanish guns of Kettle Hill and San Juan Hill were trying to stop them with puffs of rifle fire and explosions of cannon. The silence of the day was shattered forever. And Brian Dexter Cook was eyewitness to the most memorable land encounter of the Spanish-American War, in which he was to play a major role, all unknowingly.

Both white and Negro American soldiers would die this day.

But this moment, this hour, belonged to Teddy Roosevelt and the Rough Riders. The battles for Kettle Hill and San Juan Hill were intense.

The firing was ceaseless and never-ending. Rebel yells pierced the air. The bugle continued to blare, sending its battle cry across the intervening space between horsemen and defenders of the hills. Brian lowered his head, aware that two horsemen on his right had gone down, kicking and dying in the trampled dust of the passage of many horses. He thought he spotted Tex Whitover and hoped that he was wrong. He lost sight of Colonel Teddy and found Dick Davis close to his side after a tense, anxious glance. The hills suddenly steepened; the ground rose in copses of bushes, rocks and hillocks of earth. The Rough Riders swept over them like an inexorable wave. More horsemen went down, victims of the many guns before them.

A great roar was going up—a cataclysmic, concerted thunder of horses galloping, men shouting. The Rebel yell was heard again, that haunting, screeching, piercing battle cry which had sounded down the years of Civil War history and bloodshed to this very moment. It was a cry to frighten and bewilder the enemy, even a Spanish-speaking one, even these guerillas and fighters who guarded the crucial blockhouse of San Juan Hill and who ringed the top of Kettle Hill, determined to drive these *Americanos* back to the sea which had brought them here.

Brian Dexter Cook did not have to spur his mount or urge it on. Colonel Teddy had set the pace for them all. The troopers were following him in an almost instinctive, mindless gallop. But no charge anywhere was ever so purposeful or dead-set on its target. The blockhouse cresting San Juan loomed larger, nearer. Ever closer. Up front, the Colonel was a brown blur, both himself and his horse, flashing in the sunlight laden with dust. Hard on his rear and his flanks came all the rest of his command—the ex-cowboys, the ex-playboys, the ex-civilians, all united in a common gallop for a common cause.

But not even the Light Brigade in the Crimean War had escaped decimation for its suicidal if gallant charge. San Juan Hill was no exception. All about Brian Dexter Cook, horses were going down, pitching their riders; men were falling from the saddle, still fouled in their stirrups. Horses shrilled in agony as death and pain struck them in lightning flashes of time and movement. The toll on the Rough Riders was mounting. But the Colonel did not stop. He was pushing on, the men behind him, following his flashing saber as though it were a beacon in the wilderness. Brian's lungs ached. Men were still dying, falling, crying out in shock and pain—victims of unerring Spanish marksmanship. The blockhouse on San Juan Hill sent out thick clouds of smoke as its cannon roared and pounded. Huge mounds of earth erupted all about Brian. A horse whinnied in agony; a trooper called out in terror as his crumpling mount fell atop him as it went down, a rifle ball in its chest. Broad-faced, in sombreros and white pants, Spaniards could now be seen firing from behind bushes and low stumps of trees at the advancing horsemen. The chaos and confusion of battle, with its many sights and sounds, had now made a blistering arena of death of the terrain surrounding Kettle and San Juan. And the Rough Riders were at the very heart of that chaos—shooting, riding, hell-bent-for-leather to be with T.R. when he took the blockhouse.

"Charge!" came the sudden cry. "Charge the blockhouse!"

Brian felt himself and his mount carried on a

relentless forward surge. He himself was firing his carbine, from the saddle, at anything that moved before him that was wearing a sombrero. All about him were the dead and the dying. He saw men go down, hands outflung as bullets struck home. Blasted faces, bloodied bodies seemed to fill his eyes. But he held on to his nerve. The blood within him was pounding like so many drums. And Dick Davis was still alive—riding up ahead—just behind the thundering mount of Colonel Teddy, who had forsaken his saber and was now firing his big horse pistol at the scattered defenders emerging from the blockhouse to join their dead comrades strewn on the ground before them. A small knot of Rough Riders, bearing up the hill from the left flank, came galloping into view and joined T.R. in a last wholesale charge to the blockhouse. Brian caught sight of Sergeant Harkness. Harkness saw him at the same time. The grim smile on the cruel face was to stay in Brian Dexter Cook's memory forever. He knew as he knew nothing else in his lifetime that Dutch Henry had chosen this place and this moment for the hour of reckoning.

The sergeant's carbine came up in a dead line. The frosty blue eyes were almost mocking in the hazy sunlight. With Harkness, to either side of him, were Sergeant Stone and Big John Jameson. Fate could not have picked keener witnesses nor more just and loyal soldiers. The moment held— with horsemen galloping, Spaniards retreating, the

Colonel wheeling to send the troopers behind him out in a flanking movement to cover the rear of the blockhouse. Colonel Roosevelt's dusty, toothy face was crinkled in a thousand smile lines. He knew that victory was but a matter of moments away. Spanish voices were shouting in surrender—the blockhouse cannon had gone silent, mute testimony that their gunners were dead or defeated. And Sergeant Dutch Henry Harkness had picked his moment. His carbine spat smoke and noise. And just then an explosion sounded on Kettle Hill.

Brian Dexter Cook had flung up his own carbine to defend himself.

But he was not fast enough to beat Sergeant Harkness to the punch.

Only the abrupt pitching of his mount, as it stepped into a deceiving dip of ground, affected the outcome of Sergeant Harkness' treacherous deed. Brian Dexter Cook hardly knew what hit him.

Suddenly, he was falling, feeling a red-hot angry poker slam across his left temple. His skull seemed to explode as the cannons had. And then he was falling forward, sliding over the tossing mane of his mount, coming down on the hard, warm earth with an ugly sound. And then he was looking up at the sky, sensing horsemen pounding past him. He thought he heard Dick Davis cry out his name. But that might have been wishful thinking. And then he saw and heard nothing more.

The Battle of San Juan Hill had ended for Brian Dexter Cook.

With a bang. And a blinding flash of light.

He had not whimpered.

It was not his way.

The battles for the hills of San Juan and Kettle were decisive. The war turned on this one charge. For with both hills secured and the blockhouse rendered impotent, the Army could now push on to assault heavily fortified El Caney. General Garcia, emboldened by the message Lieutenant Rowan had delivered, swept down from the hills to the west, at the head of his Cuban Rebels force, and added his weight to the U.S. drive forward. El Caney fell. And Santiago's fate was sealed. There was nothing between the blockaded city and the Americans. Victory seemed so close now. Everywhere a Cuban looked, he would see a man wearing the uniform of the United States, be he soldier, sailor, marine, or Rough Rider. Old Glory was flying now over many a Spanish outpost and observation point. The *Americanos* were taking Cuba!

*Es verdad, amigos!*

It was true, friends.

Cuba's fate was sealed.

Brian Dexter Cook missed all the events of that fateful afternoon and evening. He lay in a coma, as though he were a dead man.

Sergeant Harkness' bullet had put him out of action.

He would not regain his feet for days, hovering between life and death on a hospital cot to the rear of the front lines.

He had become, all unwillingly, one of the sixteen hundred casualties the United States forces had suffered that day, culminating in their assumption of the ridges commanding Santiago. San Juan and Kettle had been the keys to that kingdom. But the price had been costly, indeed.

First Lieutenant John J. Pershing would write in his report to his superiors: *White regiments and black regiments fought shoulder to shoulder . . . unmindful of race or color . . . and mindful only of their common duty as Americans.*

Colonel Theodore Roosevelt and his Rough Riders became the talk of the world. The charge up San Juan Hill could not be topped. Not in this war, at any rate, which was now rushing towards conclusion.

Its triumphant end would only be a matter of days now.

A war that was already over for Brian Dexter Cook.

With the siege of Santiago just beginning.

Stephen Crane, too, had missed all the action at San Juan and Kettle. Delirious with fever, he was sent back to Daiquirí and placed on a ship carrying the sick and wounded away from the battle zone.

He had not found his red badge of courage. He never would.

Nor had he ever fully understood and comprehended the ugly realities of war. He had always questioned the sanity of men fighting at all.

He would die on June 5, 1900, a broken man, only twenty-nine years of age.

Immortality was his, however. Not for medals or distinguished acts of bravery. Simply for the writing of one unforgettable book about war and what it does to men.

No one who read it would ever forget *The Red Badge Of Courage*.

It was a book for the ages.

With Santiago under siege, the days that followed brought more activity and further developments. The governor of beleaguered Cuba sent an order to Admiral Cervera to try to run the blockade set up by the North Atlantic Squadron outside the harbor. This, Cervera tried to do, but all in vain. On July third, in a single file along the Cuban coast in a westerly direction, the Spanish fleet collided with the pursuing American naval vessels. Rear Admiral William T. Sampson did not give the initial orders to attack. These were rendered by Commodore Winfield Schley. No matter which officer was responsible, each and every vessel under Cervera's command was sent to the bottom or forced to beach. The Spanish Navy was no longer a factor in the Spanish-American War. Victory for the United States was a veritable cinch, as one of Brian Dexter Cook's more slangy colleagues wrote in a dispatch to his own newspaper. Nobody disagreed with him.

And as with Dewey at Manila Bay, not a single American vessel received any serious damage. Nor did any American seaman lose his life. The United States Navy once again had done itself proud. America ruled the battle waters of the theatre of war.

As for Richard Harding Davis, he performed a service that very few newspapermen would have done. When he rushed off his dispatch to the *Journal*, with his brilliant account of the Battle of San Juan Hill, he also posted a story for Brian Dexter Cook, to be sent off to Mr. Bennett's *Herald*. After all, it was the only thing he could do—had to do—what with Brian Dexter Cook lying in a hospital with his head all bandaged up like a mummy. Poor Brian. He had come as close to death as a man can. Sergeant Dutch Henry Harkness' carbine shot had grazed his left temple, leaving an ugly, blood-smeared crease through the golden-blonde hair. A fraction closer and the bullet would have torn Brian's head away. He had come that close to the Grim Reaper.

The young man would live to write some more, to love some more—perhaps cover the next war to come along, after this one ended officially. Richard Harding Davis, with true newspaperman's instinct and knowledge—as with all the other reporters covering the Spanish-American War—had chosen to designate Colonel Roosevelt's charge with the Rough Riders as the Battle of San Juan Hill. After all, the important blockhouse had been there, hadn't it?

Besides, Kettle Hill had no sound to it at all, no color, no *feel*. William Randolph Hearst gave him no argument on that.

"Well, Sergeant Harkness," Colonel Theodore Roosevelt barked in a tone of voice that brooked no further lies or hypocrisy. "I am waiting for your explanation. Make it good. There's a firing squad waiting for a man who did what you tried to do at San Juan Hill."

The first Volunteer Cavalry, now based in Santiago, with the city under military occupation by the United States Army, had earned its reprieve from battle. Roosevelt, keenly appreciative of the fruits of his victories at San Juan and Kettle, now had the distasteful affair on his hands of one of his non-commissioned officers willfully attempting to kill a newspaperman at the height of the gallant charge which had electrified both America and the world. It was fitting that the Rough Riders be billeted in one of the oldest and fanciest hotels in all Santiago. T.R. was using the largest room on the first floor for his command headquarters. It

was in this room that he had had Sergeant Dutch
Henry Harkness brought under armed guard. Two
privates stood behind Harkness, rifles at the ready.
Sergeant Harkness could no longer be trusted. Not
alone with a man like Colonel Teddy.

Dutch Henry, freshly shaved, uniform pressed
and sparkling, with his Congressional Medal of
Honor clearly visible on his broad chest, stood at
attention, heels together, arms at his side, face
trained on the fan on the ceiling. Another slowly
rotating fan like the one back at the *cantina* in
Tampa. A thousand memories ago.

"I snapped off a shot from my carbine, Colonel,"
Harkness said tonelessly. "Mr. Cook had a Spaniard
coming up on his rear with a machete—it was a
bad shot. I apologize for that."

Roosevelt snorted. "Don't bunkhouse me, Sergeant. You're the best shot in the Volunteers. And
if you think wearing your Congressional Medal is
going to sway me one way or the other—you're
mistaken." He leaned back in his chair and
drummed his right hand on the table which had
been set up for him as a desk. He shook his head.
"What was it, Harkness? A grudge dating back to
that day in Jacksonville when he knocked you
down for insulting Miss Weatherall?"

"No, sir."

"Don't lie to me. You're jealous of Brian Dexter
Cook. You have been since the day you met.
Now—I'm going to ask you once more—did you

or did you not attempt to take the life of Brian Dexter Cook?''

"No, sir."

T.R. sighed, shaking his head. "I am sorry, Harkness, that you are not man enough to own up to your dastardly act. That at least would show something. But you are lying. I have the sworn statements of two eyewitnesses. Men of your own platoon. They will testify against you at your court-martial. Two men whose records are unimpeach-able—Sergeant Stone and Private Jameson—men who were at your side all through the gallop up those hills.''

Sergeant Harkness' face was expressionless.

"I will stand by what I have said, Colonel Roosevelt."

"So you will, Harkness. And you'll go to the wall for it. But I have a much better notion." Colonel Roosevelt leaned forward in his chair. His teeth showed in a tight smile. "You're a fine soldier, Dutch Henry. You always were. A little harsh at times for my liking, but a good soldier, nonetheless. I'm not going to put this before a military court until Brian Dexter Cook is out of sick bay and up and about again. Are you follow-ing me, Sergeant Harkness?"

"Sir?" For once, the Sergeant's voice betrayed him. There was surprise and mystification in his tone.

"I'm a great Bible reader, Harkness. I believe

in the Good Book. An eye for an eye and a tooth for a tooth. I shall leave your fate to Mr. Cook. I will let him decide what satisfaction he wants. I hope to God he wants to call you out with pistols or sabers. Or nothing less than a sound thrashing. By God, sir, you have disgraced this regiment! Put a scarlet stain on its record in its finest hour. I never shall forgive you for that, Sergeant Harkness.''

The two armed privates had no expression at all on their faces. Harkness did not stir. His tall figure was as still as stone.

Wearily, sadly, Colonel Theodore Roosevelt motioned to the guards. "Take him away. Out of my sight. He will remain under detention until further orders. And hear me well—if he is missing when Mr. Cook is healthy again—I'll have both your hides for it! Now, get out—the lot of you.''

Sergeant Dutch Henry Harkness saluted stiffly, about-faced in his impeccable military manner, and marched out of the room, flanked by his rifle escort. Colonel Roosevelt stared at the door long after it had closed and then put his face in his hands. He shuddered.

There was only one thing in this whole sordid affair to be grateful for—to thank the Almighty for.

The boy had not been killed.

Had that happened, it would have been too much to bear. Even for Theodore Roosevelt. He was very fond of Brian Dexter Cook.

He fervently hoped that Theodore, Jr. would grow to be as fine a man—as talented and courageous.

He had heard from all hands how Brian Dexter Cook had distinguished himself in the charge up San Juan Hill. Dick Davis, too. Bravo for war correspondents like these two. *Bully, bully!*

Brian Dexter Cook lay abed in one of the best rooms of Santiago's main hospital. There were freshly cut flowers in a white vase, and on the plain walls hung a wooden replica of Christ on the Cross. There was no other ornamentation in the room, all white and sanitary. Silence was a characteristic that he would always associate with this place. It was like being in a church or any place of worship. The nurses were all nuns, cowled figures who hardly spoke to him as they performed their many duties. Even the doctor, a little, round-shouldered man with a sad Spanish face, was not very communicative. It was as if Cuba's fate in the war had been his own personal tragedy. But he, the conquered, never showed any malice or ill will toward Brian, one of the victors.

The nearly fatal wound which had almost cost him his life ached terribly those first thirty-six hours. There was a throbbing, ceaselessly burning sensation along the left side of his face. A hand mirror passed to him by one of the silent nuns revealed an ugly, inch-wide swath cut through the field of his golden hair, just above the ear. It was not pretty at all, and he doubted if the hair would grow back. The sad doctor assured him that it would. A few weeks, perhaps, *señor*.

There were dreams those first days and nights. And nightmares, too. Everything collided in his brain. Images of America and Lois Weatherall, Dick Davis, T.R., Dutch Henry, and Rita Sanchez— and that last violent action riding up the hills— Dutch Henry's cruel face—the raised carbine and then the hammer-blow to his skull—and falling, falling from the saddle—with guns crashing, men screaming and dying . . .

He recalled no early visitors, not even Dick Davis.

He did not know that he had been in a fever of delirium for better than two days. His life had been despaired of by all. And then, slowly, his finely tuned body, his healthy flesh and reflexes, returned to normal. His temperature leveled off. He was well again and remembering he had an appetite and a thirst. The nuns all smiled, at last, crossing themselves before the man on the cross on the wall.

And he was sitting up in his hospital bed, trying to read, attempting to reorient himself to all that was happening in the besieged world about him. Santiago had fallen—he knew that—but what else had happened? Who was going to come to him and tell him? Where was Dick?

When his room door clicked open and the figure of a nurse loomed dimly, he did not realize at first who stood there. And then he heard her unforgettable, low-pitched, cool, calm voice. The voice he remembered so well. The voice he would take to the grave with him.

"Oh, Brian . . . my dear . . ." The calmness was a hushed prayer.

The schooner cap, the aproned frock—and Miss Lois Weatherall's face materialized like something out of a dream. He blinked, shook himself, and wordlessly extended both arms. She came to him in a rush, the violet-shaded eyes streaming, the perfect mouth trembling, the cumulative impact of her beauty exploding upon all his senses . . . His heart thumped.

And then she was in his hungry arms, yielding her mouth, her lips, her heart, and her soul to him. It was a moment beyond all dreaming and expectation. It was heaven on this earth.

"Darling, darling . . ." Lois Weatherall murmured happily between kisses and whispers, "if anything had happened to you . . ."

Brian Dexter Cook kissed her again. Ardently, lovingly. A kiss that would last a lifetime. The war and all that had occurred was nothing but a bad dream. Now was only love and Miss Lois Weatherall.

\*　　\*　　\*

She was more woman than he would ever know. If he had had any doubts about that at all, they evaporated in the next few breathless minutes. She had risen to her feet, silently gone to the room door, and locked it. When she turned and looked across the room at him in the bed, he saw something in her eyes he had never seen before. There was smokiness to the violet-shaded orbs; her red mouth was slightly parted, and her full bosom was heaving. "Brian—" she whispered with a catch in her throat. "I don't want to wait any longer . . . not anymore. . . . If this is being bad, then I'm bad . . . but God knows how I feel about you . . ."

He could only gaze at her in wonder as she returned to the bed. He watched her slender, graceful hands plucking at the uniform she wore. He tried to think, tried to stop her, but he couldn't. Waves of uncontrollable hunger were sweeping over him, washing him in a flood tide of unbridled desire. She unbuttoned her blouse, opened it, and suddenly it was away from her, revealing the lovely young bosom. And when she stepped out of her skirt and stood before him in one swift exposure of all her womanly charms, he was done. He reached for her blindly, and she lowered herself to his arms, her hungry mouth biting into his own. "Oh, darling . . . this can't be wrong . . . not the way I feel about you . . ."

Her warm breath fanned at him. His stomach convulsed.

But still he tried to fight back, to be the gentleman.

"Lois, for God's sake, we mustn't do this—not yet—"

"Hush," she said gently, the stronger of the two, as most women are the very first time. "If you had died out there, then this would never have been. . . . I'm not going to risk that, darling—not again. . . . I love you, Brian Dexter Cook. I love you as I have never loved anyone before."

"I know, I know," he murmured, pressing his lips into the forest of her long dark hair. His hands were over her, roving, touching, feeling, finding her for *real* now. Not guessing, not imagining, not fumbling like a schoolboy on his first date. Her nearness, her closeness, was a flaming torch touching off so many fires within him.

"Do you love me, Brian?" This last so close to his ear.

"Oh, God, yes! . . . Do I ever! . . ."

"Then make love to me, darling, before it's too late again . . ."

Her arms went around his neck. She had never worn corsets or stays or girdles. She had never needed them. And Brian's hospital smock was all that stood between him and her warm, waiting flesh. Her hands pulled at the smock, rolling it upward past his waist. And then her cool fingers reached down and found him, closed over him with a low, happy, feminine sigh that spoke vividly of what she truly wanted. His temples throbbed, and even the dull ache on the left side vanished in a torrent of delirious joy and excitement. His loins rioted.

He drew her toward him, turning her slowly, and when he mounted her waiting body, he had never known such happiness and total reality. The splendid thighs beneath him parted; he reached for her, going at her firmly and yet tenderly. She seemed to move upward to meet him, melding herself to him and melting like warm syrup to his gentle invasion of her innermost recesses. And then he was beyond desire and control. He was a feverish, yearning, plunging, pushing man who wanted to please his woman. Which he did in a thoroughly manful way.

The newness of her, the secret insides of her overwhelmed him.

She was running mountain streams; a warm, bubbling brook; a pleasant glade of grass; a laughing, rippling fountain of life. She was all things to him and everything. Never had he felt so complete, so happy. So very much loved and in love.

She clung to him as if she never wanted to let him go.

He looked at her, his face inches from her own, and marveled.

The cameo features, the tilted chin, the violet-shaded eyes, the long, dark, damply glistening hair—where had cool and collected Lois Weatherall gone? This lovely, passionate wanton in his arms was an exotic stranger. A woman of vast charms— who knew how to use them.

"Shameless hussy," he breathed into her hair, dreamily.

"Yes," she whispered back. "Isn't it wonderful?"

"I love you, Miss Weatherall," he pledged with all his heart.

"I love you, Mr. Cook. So never let me go."

The Spanish-American War which had begun in the last week of April was barely ninety days old. It would last a grand total of one hundred and thirteen days—one of the shortest wars in the history books. Perhaps it was also the shortest in terms of historical significance.

But the other war, the private war, between Brian Dexter Cook and Lois Weatherall had already ended. For good and all.

On a hospital bed behind a locked door in a patient's room in a hospital in Santiago. In mid-July of eighteen hundred and ninety-eight.

The man on the cross on the plain white wall looked down at them.

Lois Weatherall was certain in her heart that he was smiling. Brian Dexter Cook knew he was. There could be no wrong in what they had done. Brian had found his true love.

# HAVANA AND HEARTACHES

With the victorious American troops marching through the streets of Cuban cities, villages, and towns on their way to Havana, there was not only the drum and the bugle to measure their trampling feet. Many a time the troops would break into song. The war was almost over and everyone was happy with the knowledge that soon they would be sailing back to America. "Green Grow The Lilacs" was the most universally sung melody. No one knew why—it simply worked out that way. But the popular ballad was destined to give all Americans a name—a tag, a label—which would continue forever. "Here come the green-grows," the Cubans and Spaniards would announce derisively. And somehow this became bastardized as *gringo*. And from these days forward, throughout the Latin world—Cuba, Mexico, Central and South America, Spain—people from America would always and ever be designated as *gringos*. Often it was a disparaging term, But no American soldier or sailor or marine really cared.

Stateside was beckoning. It was only a matter of weeks now.

Some people, however, had some unfinished business to attend to.

The Army was mopping up in Cuba, negotiating with the Spanish government for a true and lasting peace. Hostilities had virtually ceased, save for sporadic encounters with last-ditch guerillas who refused to surrender. Colonel Roosevelt and the Rough Riders lent their riding and shooting skills to this nuisance, and only a few minor outbursts that were swiftly crushed caused them any trouble. Meanwhile, others had to see to their own loose ends to tie up in a neat and tidy parcel. One of these was Brian Dexter Cook, reporter for the New York *Herald*, a man whom Colonel Roosevelt was recommending for a medal, in conjunction with his famous colleague, Richard Harding Davis of the *Journal*. Both men had served gallantly with the First Volunteer Cavalry.

The Rough Riders admired and loved them both, for their part in the Cuban campaign, their bravery under fire.

"I thought Davis and Cook were just paraders until I bunked, faced fire, and ate beans out of the same can with them. Now I want to hear nothing against them in my presence," snapped one veteran.

Dick Davis had moved on by ship to cover the brief invasion of Puerto Rico. U.S. troops were heading for the Philippines to block any Spanish interference there. When Brian had made his good-byes to Dick Davis before he left Havana, there was only one thought on the mind of the most famous war correspondent in America.

"See here, Brian. Why not let this business with Dutch Henry Harkness slide? Let the Army shoot him for you. He richly deserves it."

"No, Dick. This is between the two of us. We'll settle it like gentlemen. T.R. gave me the right to do as I wish."

"Harkness is no gentleman. You know that."

"Just the same—"

"Well, fool that you are, farewell. I wish you the best, however you intend to get your own back. Be warned. Whatever you choose—Dutch Henry will not fight fairly."

"I know," Brian smiled warmly at his greatest

friend. "See you in the good old U.S. of A. some day soon. I intend to get back there as soon as possible. And thanks again for writing my San Juan Hill story while I was under the weather. I won't forget that."

"I don't intend that you should. When we meet in Delmonico's, the drinks are on you, my boy. Perhaps Steve Crane will be well by then."

"Done." They shook hands warmly. Then embraced briefly.

Richard Harding Davis picked up his traveling bag, smiled, and said, "Give my best regards to Miss Weatherall, won't you?"

With that, he was gone.

And part of the life and the fun and the excitement went out of Cuba. But Brian Dexter Cook caught hold of himself and set his chin. There was still Sergeant Harkness to see to.

Even though Miss Lois Weatherall heartily disapproved of such goings-on between grown men: sportsmanship, the Code—*duels* in this day and age! Why, it was medieval, that's what it was!

She had no love at all for Sergeant Harkness and couldn't care less what happened to him. But she did care what happened to Brian Dexter Cook. Now that they were in love—truly in love.

She didn't want to lose him after spending so many years finding him. If anything were to happen to him now . . .

She didn't want to think about that.

She *wouldn't* think about that.

It was too awful to consider.


"Ready, Dutch Henry?"

"Just about."

"Come on, then—everybody's waiting on you. Especially that Cook gentleman." The turnkey opened the iron door, yawning.

It was a very private affair. It had to be. Army regulations forbade such things as the settling of grievances with fists or weapons. But it was an old Army custom dating back to the Revolutionary War. What could not be settled by a Court of Inquiry—or rather what must be kept from such a tribunal—could be secretly resolved in this fashion. So it was that Sergeant Dutch Henry Harkness left his cell in the early morning hours of a day in late July and prepared to square accounts with one Brian Dexter Cook. Colonel Theodore Roosevelt knew the fight was coming off, privately approved, and deeply regretted his absence that day. He was wanted at Army headquarters to discuss the coming invasion of Puerto Rico. But his heart and his hopes rested on Brian Dexter Cook. He was positive Brian would give Harkness more than he himself would receive.

The challenge was fisticuffs, bared. The arena was the empty stable behind the old stone building which was temporarily housing the second squad

of the fourth platoon of the First Cavalry—those
volunteers with whom Brian had gone up San Juan
Hill—Whitover, Cody, Stone, Jameson, Indian Joe
Jones, and all that bunch. They all sat waiting
now, ringing the battle area in a perimeter of
defense. Spectators all. Harkness could not escape,
even if he bested Brian Dexter Cook. Which was
doubted by all, once they saw the young reporter
stripped down to his trousers. His torso was lithe,
bronzed, and very muscular. His demeanor was
grim and unsmiling. Only the cruel welt across his
temple, where the hair was growing back now,
was even remotely a sign that this was a man who
had lived and dared and been through adventures
and scrapes and hard times.

The stable was respectfully silent as Dutch Henry
Harkness strolled in, his armed escort of two
riflemen stepping back to give him room to swing.
Harkness quickly and silently took off his blue
denim prison shirt. His cruel face and slit-eyed
smile was taunting as he glared across the room at
Brian Dexter Cook. The challenger, the man who
would be revenged for the episode on San Juan
Hill. Miss Weatherall was nowhere to be seen.
Mercifully, Brian had kept all the details of the
match from her. Time enough to tell her when it
was all over, whatever the outcome. Sergeant Stone,
gray-haired and distinguished for one so young,
was to be the referee. He stepped forward now,

unsmiling. Brian and Harkness crossed from their sides of the stable to join him.

"Marquis of Queensbury rules, gentlemen. No butting, no fingers in the eyes, no striking below the waistline." The resonant voice was almost toneless. "You will fight until one man goes down and stays down. There will be no rounds this time. Agreed?"

Both men nodded, never taking their eyes off one another.

Stone murmured, "And I will shoot you on the spot, Dutch Henry, if you try any of your mean, low tricks with this man."

Harkness showed his teeth and said nothing. He was a very formidable-looking opponent. The sergeant's frame was lean, hard, broad-shouldered. Not an ounce of fat on him.

The men ringing them, giving both fighters a clearance of no more than twenty feet, were muttering impatiently now, wanting the fight to start. There had been wagering beyond belief, and despite Harkness' unpopularity, more than one volunteer had bet on him to win. Loyalty was one thing, wagering quite another—but Brian Dexter Cook did not care. This was what he wanted. A chance to beat Dutch Henry face-to-face, toe-to-toe. To ram his lies and his many cruelties right down his throat. Sergeant Stone drew back: "May the best man win. And if there is any justice or a

God, the best man will.'' With that, he took up his position some five feet from the combatants.

Everyone in the stable, standing, crouching, squatting on bales of ancient hay, began to murmur louder, talking it up. The signal for the start of the encounter was to be the clanging of the iron triangle that usually symbolized Mess Call, apart from a bugle. It sounded now, held aloft by a beaming, expectant Tex Whitover. The former Texas Ranger who had survived San Juan Hill, despite Brian's fear that he hadn't, was plumb anxious to see Dutch Henry get his ears pinned back. Young Cook was the one to do it—Whitover was sure of that. He knew men—this young reporter was the goods, right enough! Snakes who tried to kill one of their own in the heat of battle were the real sinners of this world, according to John ''Tex'' Whitover.

The come-and-get-it triangle clanged noisily.

The fight was under way.

Brian Dexter Cook and Dutch Henry Harkness moved toward each other. Warily. Circling. Like chicken hawks ready for the kill.

The voices of the spectators rose in unison, exhorting action, suggesting caution to the chosen fighter of their bet—it was a ceremony and ritual as old as time itself.

The atmosphere of the stable, a combination of decayed manure and grimy walls and men's closeness and the heat of the dawning day, all combined to charge the air with tension. And excitement.

Harkness' frosty blue eyes measured Brian's handsome face across the horizon of his two bony-knuckled fists.

"Pretty Boy," he breathed through his clenched teeth and shot out a savage right hand. Brian parried and danced back, feinting with his left hand all the way. Harkness closed in on him. He was a deceptive fighter, Dutch Henry, seeming almost indolent and careless, and then—he moved, with cobra-swiftness. Brian's head snapped back as Harkness' right fist thudded into his jaw. A shout went up and then subsided. Brian had answered back with a deft one-two combination. The one found Harkness' lean middle; the second blow landed hard on the sergeant's blunt jaw. Now both men had drawn blood, but each was still standing on his own two feet. Nothing had been gained by either, save the testing of one another's punches. They had been painful.

They circled each other again. Their expressions had changed. No longer were they calm, cool, and collected. Dutch Henry was breathing hard through his nose; Brian was feeling the blood singing in his veins. He ached to punish this man who stole kisses and telescopes and shot at companions in arms with intent to kill. He lowered his head, dancing expertly toward the sergeant in the style and manner which had won him credits at Cornell on the boxing team. If they could see him now—brawling in a stable like any uneducated oaf on Saturday night.

But this was different. This was for honor, himself, and a woman—three things that mattered, if he was going to go on living. With himself and everyone else.

It was a gentleman's code, perhaps, but the only code for him. Father and Mother would have understood and approved if they were still alive. He knew that as surely as he knew his own name and that he loved Lois Weatherall and hated men like Dutch Henry Harkness.

Brian was brought back to the present by a vicious, jarring punch to his middle. He fell back, Harkness following after him, flailing with both hands now. Right, left, right, left, and then right again. He took nearly all those punches but escaped damage because his footwork was still as deft and expert as ever. His half-turned body absorbed less punishment. Harkness' breathing was hoarse and strained now, and Brian knew his man was tiring. A good sign. He had paced his own efforts and would last longer that way, but he, too, was impatient for the kill. The sergeant's sweaty, taut face was a temptation difficult to bypass. As early as it was in the fight—

So he teased Harkness with a poking left hand that did not quite land. The sergeant backed off. Brian pressed the advantage. Behind his target, he could see the Rough Riders, their faces a haze of many different expressions. He did not pause to sort them out. Dutch Henry was the only face he was interested in. He found that face now—bobbing unprotected above the lowered fists, for one instant. He took that instant and used it well.

He drove a deadly from-the-shoulder right hand and it caught the sergeant flush in the face. Blood spurted as Harkness' nose and lips received most of the blow. Brian closed in, alternating his left and right hands. He knew he had the tall Dutch Henry on the run now. It was only a matter of time. The stable enclosure rang with cheers and shouts as everyone sensed the moment of decision very close.

But everyone was wrong, including Brian Dexter Cook.

No one, even those who knew him best, who had served with him these last months, had reckoned on the guile and brute cunning of Dutch Henry Harkness. He caught everyone by surprise in the next few flashing seconds. Most of all, the man with whom he was fighting.

As Brian boxed him into a corner of the cleared area, literally tattooing him with a succession of accurate punches, the sergeant made his move—a totally unexpected one and exactly what he had been warned about. Sergeant Louis Stone saw it coming, but even he was too late to stop the illegal action. It was something back-alley fighters and

street-fighters excelled in and had no compunc-
tions about employing as a ploy to win brawls.
Brian Dexter Cook did not have a chance.

Harkness's right leg came up, with Brian barely
a foot away. The bony knee, a battering ram of
power, rammed into Brian's abdomen. A killing
blow. One that drove the younger man backwards,
doubling him up in bursting agony, his hands coming up reflexively to paw at the area of trouble.
His guard was down and Harkness had all the
opening he wanted. As bruised and battered as he
was from Brian's expert pounding, Harkness' face
transformed into a bloody but gleeful mask. A
snarl erupted from his throat, a deep animal sound,
barely human. He rushed, head lowered, all lean
one hundred and eighty pounds of him thrusting
forward in a pile-driving lunge. Brian was trapped,
stumbling in contorted agony before him. The
sergeant's head made contact with his middle once
more and Brian Dexter Cook went down—victim
of a man who had not fought like a gentleman or
obeyed Marquis of Queensbury rules.

It all happened so fast, so furiously, that every
man surrounding the fighters was powerless to act.
And Harkness was savage now. Heedless, mindless.
A bloodied brute who only knew that his enemy
was down, sprawled in the dust before him,
defenseless, at his mercy. It did not matter how
one won, only that one *did* win. The methods were

unimportant. A man facing a court-martial, and a firing squad perhaps, no matter how this thing came out, behaves instinctively. The law of the jungle, the survival of the fittest. Man-made rules and codes of behavior had never meant anything to Sergeant Dutch Henry Harkness, anyway. As they didn't now.

He reached Brian in those frozen seconds when no one seemed able to stop him. He raised a booted foot above Brian Dexter Cook's head. Brian was trying to rise, his face a rictus of agony, his blue eyes perfectly aware of what Harkness was planning for him. And he knew he'd be unable to move fast enough to get out of the way. The blows to his stomach had completely knifed him— stabbing blades of burning pain had taken over his insides—

"Pretty boy—" Sergeant Harkness hissed and brought the heavy foot downward toward Brian's face. It loomed in Brian's eyes like a juggernaut of destruction. He tried to get out of the way. He never would have been in time to do so—

A shot thundered in the split-second silence that had engulfed the stable and all those present.

One blasting, thunderous sound of gunfire which seemed to roll and reverberate around the wooden walls.

Everyone was stunned by the explosion.

And everyone saw what this one single shot accomplished.

Sergeant Dutch Henry Harkness' face came apart with wonder and surprise. The heavy boot that was traveling downward to crush Brian Dexter Cook's handsome face to jelly with its hob-nailed surface now angled to one side. Harkness staggered, trying to look down at himself to see where the bullet had gone in, to understand what was happening to him. He never did find out, nor did he see the widening, crimson splotch that suddenly blossomed on his lean, sweaty chest. An ugly vermilion spider just over his heart. The spider crawled slowly across his pulsing flesh.

The sergeant's right foot came down, and he followed it to the floor of the stable—pitching forward on his face, without so much as a murmur of sound. He lay very still, his long arms outflung, as if in supplication for mercy. There was none for him here.

All eyes in that stable swung instinctively toward the direction of the pistol shot. They were all experienced combat troops. They knew how to pinpoint the source of a bullet. Brian Dexter Cook looked up, baffled, hurt, still trying to pull himself together.

John "Tex" Whitover spun the frontier model Colt .45 in his right hand and deftly replaced it in the leather holster on his hip—his rangy body shrugged; his lined, weather-beaten face almost indifferent. Sergeant Louis Shepherd Stone, hands hanging in mute inaction, muttered: "Whitover, you damn fool. I could have stopped Dutch Henry—"

"No, you couldn't," Whitover snapped. " 'Sides, I heard you say you'd shoot him if he turned dirty like he did."

Stone shook himself and reached down to help Brian Dexter Cook to his feet. None of the Rough Riders had found their voices yet. It was all so sudden, so incredible—and now morning sunlight was filtering through the windows and the many cracks in the walls of the stable. Someone, at last, rasped, "If this don't beat all—"

"He had it coming. He was a mean bastard," another replied. This was no one but Private Riddle, the man who had witnessed the very first punch ever exchanged between Sergeant Harkness and Mr. Cook.

Nobody had moved to see if Dutch Henry Harkness was alive. They all knew a dead man when they saw one. They had been in battle.

Big John Jameson clenched his fists and looked worried.

"T.R. will nail our hides to the barn door when he gets wind of this. Even if Dutch Henry did have it coming, it won't look good."

Tex Whitover, jaws moving slowly on a chaw of tobacco as he watched Stone administer to Brian Dexter Cook, had an answer for that, too.

"None of you is thinking right. We saved a firing squad a heap of trouble and a lot of fuss and bother. Harkness was no saint; not a drop of good or Christian charity in his bones. The boy here was dusting his feathers real good and he played dirty. You all saw him. You're witnesses—he was begging for the slug I put into him."

"Nice shot, Tex," Brian Dexter Cook smiled, as feeble as he felt. No matter how this thing turned out, he was so damn glad to be alive and all in one piece. Harkness' boot would have ruined him forever.

"Nothing at all for a Texas Ranger, son," said Tex Whitover, grinning, "and a rootin', tootin', shootin' Rough Rider."

A statement which just about said it all.

For every man present.

And for Brian Dexter Cook, the newspaperman from Manhattan, New York.

Everyone was cheering now.

It was like winning the Spanish-American War.

Later that day, Lois Weatherall heard the account of the terrible fight. Brian told her all the details as they strolled through a garden behind the Church of St. Agnes. Havana was beautiful at this time of year, and the war was truly dwindling down. August was near, and the negotiations between Spain and the United States were reaching fulfillment. Seldom had any conflict been so thoroughly covered by the newspapers of the world. The *Journal*, the *Herald*, the *World*, the *Baltimore Sun*, and hundreds of dailies all over America had done their job and done it well—not to mention the thousands of tabloids in Europe and Asia and South America and Great Britain combined.

"Brian, you could have been killed."

"I wasn't. Thanks to Tex Whitover."

"I'm going to kiss that man when next I see him."

"Don't. He wouldn't like it. Besides, he's always got a plug of tobacco in his jaws."

They both laughed. They were happy young lovers who had found each other in a universe of strangers, young lovers for whom everything seemed very golden and bright and promising for the future.

There was a stone bench with creeping vines near the mission wall. They sat down, their hands intertwined. Brian Dexter Cook would never cease marveling at the beauty of Lois Weatherall. The eyes, the nose, the chin, the lips—the ivory skin without a blemish—what a portrait she was. Any artist would have given his eye teeth to have her sit for him. He promised himself that that was the first thing he would do for her when they returned to New York. No Charles Dana Gibson for her. Merrick of Fifth Avenue was the man for the job.

She nestled her head against his shoulder. The glorious fresh fragrance of her filled his nostrils. He kissed her cheek and considered all that was good in this life. The blaze of battle at Las Guasimas, San Juan, Kettle, and all the other battles seemed remote and far away now. Now was only Miss Lois Weatherall.

And making plans for their future together.

"What about Mr. William Randolph Hearst?" he asked suddenly.

"What about him?" she murmured from the bulwark of his shoulder.

"Well, now that you're mustered out of the nursing profession and you plan to become Mrs. Brian Dexter Cook and I fully intend to keep you busy having lots of children, well—"

"Well?" she teased.

"Well, one reporter in a family is enough, isn't it? Bennett was very pleased with my work here in Cuba and has offered me the sort of deal only the Dick Davises get. We can live very nicely on ten thousand a year, I should think."

"Yes. That is a tidy amount."

"You haven't answered me yet," he reminded her, still staring straight ahead at the garden wall. She had not moved her head from his shoulder. "Lois, please tell me what you have decided. I know you made quite a stir with your dispatches back stateside—woman's point of view and all that—but the man must carry the load in a family. You can see that, can't you?''

"Quite true, Mr. Cook. And you are correct.''

"Then you're saying? . . .''

"I am saying that yes, I will end my association with Mr. Hearst, yes, I will marry you, and yes, I want to have lots and lots of babies. But I must tell you, Mr. Brian Dexter Cook, I am not going to give up my writing. It means too much to me.''

"Lois—'' He turned her gently toward him. He had to look into the violet-shaded eyes, those incredible eyes. "Of course, I don't want you to give that up. You write very well—''

"Oh, thank you, kind sir.''

"Stop clowning, darling. You know I want only what you want.''

"Do you want to write a book, Brian Dexter Cook?''

He blinked. "Book—you mean—''

"Yes. *I'm* going to write a book. It may take me years but that's what I intend to do. While I'm having—and during—all those babies. A book about me, you, Mr. Roosevelt, and the Rough Riders and this awful war that took so many lives of so many men and boys.''

"That's a lovely idea, Lois. Go to it. I will be cheering every page of the way.''

"I know you will, dearest. That's one of the many reasons why I love you, Brian.''

"Not half as much as I love you, Lois Weatherall."

They kissed, their lips meeting in a Spanish garden in Havana, while all about them the world readied itself to clear up the sad but necessary business of America's first global war—the war which would make the United States a major world power.

Overhead, a swallow flew, chirping sweetly.

Higher than that, blue skies, white clouds, and a warm sun glowed.

A child's kite fluttered in the cool breezes from somewhere beyond the garden wall. It was a peaceful sight.

Brian Dexter Cook knew, with all his heart and soul and spirit, that when children can still fly kites, there will always be hope for mankind. And womankind, too.

Nothing could ever destroy that. Nothing on God's green earth.

"Lois—"

"Yes, Brian?"

"When we get back to New York and see Dick Davis again, we all must meet at Delmonico's. I'll buy you the biggest, fanciest dinner you ever set your eyes on. And then we'll go to Broadway and catch Miss Lillian Russell if she's still playing—"

"Brian, Brian."

"What's the matter? Did I say something wrong?"

"No, Brian. You never could—and you never will, I think."

Miss Lois Weatherall was right about that, too.

Brian Dexter Cook was a very rare young man, indeed.

*Bully* for him, as Teddy Roosevelt would say.

The ultimate accolade.

## Postscript to Cuba

In September of that memorable year, with autumn leaves falling in Central Park, Miss Linda Balfour, one Sunday morning, ensconced in Uncle Waldo Friedlinger's sumptuous Fifth Avenue residence, was reading the Sunday morning edition of the New York *Journal*. As all young ladies of her position and disposition were inclined to turn at once to the society page of William Randolph Hearst's eminent newspaper, she did so. Uncle Waldo, seated on the other side of the sunny parlor ruminating over a filled glass of scotch and water, heard his beautiful niece gasp. He looked up, alarmed. Linda looked as pale as death.

"What in the name of blue blazes—"

"Uncle, look!"

Uncle Waldo Friedlinger grunted. It couldn't be anything about the damned war. The war was over, and good riddance to it. Stocks had once more climbed back up to a respectable level.

"Thunderation, Linda. You know I can't see from here to there. Bring the blasted paper here if you want me to see anything in it."

This she did, with racing feet. Grunting again, he swept the newspaper from her trembling fingers and glanced down at what he held. For a moment, he was baffled; then something familiar caught his eye. A face from the past. A smiling, handsome, golden-haired lad in a Prince Albert coat. He was standing on the steps of some church or other with a truly exquisite-looking female at his side. A wedding snapshot, of course, but—the news item beneath the picture captured his attention. He shot a glance at his pallid niece once more and then lowered his gaze to the *Journal* again.

Each and every one of the words now hit home:

### WAR CORRESPONDENT
### AND MISS COOK
### ARE WED
Famous Couple United In
Double-Ring Ceremony

*Mr. Brian Dexter Cook, a foreign correspondent for James Gordon Bennett's* Herald, *was married yesterday to Miss Lois Weatherall. The bride and groom, who make their home in this city, plan a honeymoon in Havana, Cuba, where both served with honor in the recent conflict between Spain and the United States. The wedding was performed at the Marble Collegiate Church. Mr. Richard Harding Davis gave the bride away . . .*

Uncle Waldo Friedlinger did not care to read any further. He flung the paper to the parquet floor and glared at his favorite niece, who still stood before him, still trembling and very pale.

"Well," he growled, "what of it? What of them? Infernal muckrackers, warmongerers! Let them all get married—to each other! What's that got to do with any of us?"

Miss Lois Balfour smiled wanly down at him.

There was a look in her eyes that Waldo Friedlinger would never have understood. Not if he lived to be a thousand.

"Oh, Uncle," Linda Balfour sighed, "if only I had let him kiss me that day—"

"Over my dead body, young lady," Waldo Friedlinger snarled.

Disgruntled, he turned away from his niece and returned to the serious business of drinking.

Privately, he had to admit to one truth. Young Cook and his lady made a very lovely couple.

A lovely couple, indeed. Damn their eyes!

They belonged right on top of a wedding cake.

Top hat, bridal dress, and all.


And in the house on West Eighty-Second Street, around the corner from the Museum of Natural History, Mrs. Lanigan was also admiring the handsome couple pictured on the society page of the New York *Journal*.

A broken leg had kept the doughty boarding house owner from attending the church services. Still, Mrs. Lanigan had sent a basket of flowers and her very best wishes. She would never forget Miss Lois Weatherall and Mr. Brian Dexter Cook. Valentines that they were! The pair of them—like sweethearts out of a story book.

When one of her boarders, an elderly lady named Ada Kropowski, came into the cheery parlor to see how she was doing, Mrs. Lanigan proudly held up the *Journal*, spreading its pages in her hands.

"Look, Mrs. Kropowski—the darlin's got their picture in the paper. Come see—"

Mrs. Kropowski, a widow of many years, did as she was told and, nodding, sighed approvingly. "God be with them—they are nice looking, Mrs. Lanigan. It must have been a beautiful wedding."

The landlady smiled and all her freckles seemed

to come into focus. She closed the newspaper slowly, shaking her head.

"Lord, but they are goin' to have beautiful children . . ."

And they did.

Three boys and one fine girl.

The boys would be christened Richard Harding Cook, Theodore Roosevelt Cook, and Brian Dexter Cook, Jr.

The girl would be named Nellie Bly Cook.

Mr. and Mrs. Brian Dexter Cook were, whatever else, hopeless romantics.